SEA SPRAY

Sea Spray

A musician's journey of love and loss on the road to redemption

DENIS R. GRAY

For Sanae

CONTENTS

| 1 |

Despondent

He sat hunched in the late-night diner, staring blankly at the fried chicken on his plate. A dusty, fluorescent ceiling light buzzed and blinked above his head. Using a plastic fork, he moved the fries about, watching them drown in a mixture of oil and fatty bird tissue. The rain tapped on the glass window and he shut his weary eyes. Exhaustion, fatigue, tiredness….Nathan Baxter had 'em all and he was spent. He started to sob - quietly at first, then a little louder, loud enough for the waitress to glance up from the magazine she was reading. He cleared his throat, faked a smile, and got to his feet. After paying the bill he hurried out of the cafe. 'Nat', which his folks and close friends affectionately called him, was going through a divorce and custody battle for his six year old daughter Hanna. It was a one-two punch which had rocked his world. His former wife Amber had also once used that playful pet name, but nowadays, coldly referred to Nathan as 'him'.

After purchasing two bottles of beer from the grocery store, he walked slowly back to his house, pausing a couple of times to shake the rain from his umbrella. As he slid the key in the front door, he could hear his cat Checkers greet him with a barrage of loud meowing. Nat scattered some dry, fish-scented pellets into her bowl and then watched as the black and white moggie hungrily devoured the food.

'Sorry I'm late,' he said, scratching the cat's head with his index finger. As Checkers crunched her way through the snacks, Nat gathered up the beer and shuffled to the lounge room. He pushed the power button on his beloved Hi-Fi, and the greenish-blue light emanating from the front panel of the Sanyo DC640 softly illuminated the room. Lifting the head-shell, he moved the tonearm and slowly lowered the stylus onto the spinning record. It was Eric Clapton's *461 Ocean Boulevard* - a long time black vinyl friend of Nat's and one of his favourite albums.

He collapsed back into the sofa before wrenching open a beer. Nat gulped down the lager, then wiped his mouth with his sleeve. He closed his eyes and thought of Hanna, his little angel. Warm memories of 'afternoon tea' in her cubby house, 'robot rides' (where she'd balance on his feet as they walked) and the 'this little piggy' nursery rhyme all came rushing back. He smiled. The sound of her laughter and exuberant giggles filled his head. He took another swig. He wondered how Hanna's day at school was. He pondered what she'd eaten for 'big lunch' - a concern of his until recently, as he'd taken great delight in packing her daily lunch. The smile faded and his head dropped. 'How on earth did it come to this?' he sighed. Baxter's eyes grew heavy as Clapton's voice on the sorrowful 'Give Me Strength' filled the room.

A low sounding rumble, coupled with a constant 'click-click-click' sound, stirred from the speakers, waking Nat from his sleep. The auto-return mechanism on his Hi-Fi was kaput, meaning the tonearm on the record player would not release when an album had finished playing. *I really gotta get that fixed,* he thought, glancing at his wrist watch. Six-thirty. Baxter staggered to the shower and stood motionless, allowing the warm streams of water to work their magic.

As the food cupboard contained only three packets of spaghetti and an old can of fruit salad, breakfast options were limited. So, with his hair still wet, Nat fed Checkers, pulled on his leather jacket and hurried out of the house. He checked the letterbox then nodded and smiled at the elderly neighbour as she watered her flowerbed.

'They're looking great,' he offered, pointing at her purple petunias. She returned the smile.   Arriving at the bus stop just as the #74 approached, Nat boarded, paid the driver for a ticket, and found a seat at the rear of the vehicle. The journey to South Fletcher High School, his place of employment for nearly four years, took forty minutes - half an hour with no traffic. Nat removed his jacket and shaped it into a pillow, before wedging it between his shoulder and the window. He rested his head against the rumpled leather and shut his eyes as the bus groaned along the road. After a few minutes he began to feel drowsy, however loud music playing nearby roused him from his sleep. Baxter was a music teacher and had been playing guitar since he was ten. As a teenager, he'd been in a garage band called The Nighthawks, but (as he'd written, sung and composed most of their repertoire), they later changed their name to Nathan and The Nighthawks. Apart from playing high school dances, Nathan and The Nighthawks also took the honors in a local 'battle of the bands' competition. First prize was a studio session and a cheque for $100, all of which went towards releasing their very own 7" single. 'Pristine Heart' was the A-Side, with 'Vanilla Stars' on the B-Side. Both songs were written by Nathan and he was very proud of them. 'Vanilla Stars' was a poem he'd penned when he was sixteen, and a definite nod to the psychedelic '60s.

Nat looked around the bus, trying to determine the source of the music and where it was coming from. He recognised the guitar riff, and picked the song as *Ebony Eyes* by Bob Welch. Two seats away to his left, sat a skinny teenage boy in a black tee-shirt with curly, shoulder-length hair. Wrapped around the top of his head, were a pair of headphones with foam pads which sat snugly over his ears. Underneath these circular cushion pads were speakers, from which Nathan could hear the music playing. Baxter recognised the kid as one of his students - Jamie Nesbitt. Intrigued with this new audio device, Nat tapped Jamie on the shoulder and half-smiled. The kid looked around, and after recognising his music teacher, sat upright.

'Oh, hey, Mr. Baxter,' he said, surprised. 'How are you?'

'I'm doing OK, Jamie,' he replied with a nod. 'But I heard the music playing and had to ask, *what exactly is that you've got on your head?*'

'Oh, this,' answered Jamie, holding up the portable cassette player. 'It's called a Walkman.' he added before pressing the stop button on Bob Welch. 'My Dad was in Japan last month on a business trip and brought it back for me. Radical, huh?' he said, holding up the Walkman to the light before handing it to his teacher.

'Radical indeed,' replied Nat, looking over the shiny device. He ejected the cassette and read over the song titles. 'Y'know, Bob Welch was in Fleetwood Mac, don't you?

'Really?' replied Jamie.

'Uh-huh,' confirmed Baxter. He left just before they hit it really big.' Nat re-slotted the cassette in the player and then passed the Walkman back to Jamie. 'Thanks for the chat. I'll see you in class.'

Music was Nat's life, and he felt buoyant for the remainder of the journey. *Man, I gotta get my hands on a Walkman* he thought, as they neared the working-class neighbourhood of South Fletcher. When the bus pulled up at the school, Baxter made his way to the doors and descended from the vehicle.

By 1:00PM however, Baxter's buoyant mood was all but deflated. His last class before lunch was a shambles, with unruliness replacing any talk of guitar chord progressions. Nat was an accomplished musician and teacher, but a weak disciplinarian - something his ex-wife used to remind him about.

'You should be tougher and not so weak,' she would say. The memory of Amber scolding him made him smirk. *'Better to be soft and loved than hard and feared.'* he thought. Sure, he knew he was a softie but, that's who he was. He hated

violence and avoided violent movies; he stayed clear of fights, and even arguing would make him feel nauseous. That's not to say he was a pushover, but he preferred a dove to a hawk or an eagle, if that makes sense. Consequently, one or two rowdy students from his eighth-grade class would often try and test him. Today was one of those days, where the kids who *didn't* want to learn soured the mood for those who *did.* Baxter held his nerve throughout the lesson, but was pleased to hear the bell ring for lunch.

When he entered the staff room, he smiled at the school principal, Terry Bek, who had the phone to his ear while eating a finger bun. Terry returned the smile. Baxter opened the door to a small white refrigerator and removed the milk container. He gave it a quick whiff to ensure it was fresh, then picked up a coffee mug from the nearby sink. Feeling lethargic, he walked over to the drip coffee machine, hoping that the caffeine would give him a charge. As he poured the strong black coffee into his mug he heard the phone being returned to the receiver.

'No lunch again today?' Terry asked. Nat smirked and shook his head.

'Some days, I'm lucky if I remember my name,' he replied.

Terry was a few years older than Nathan, and aware that his music teacher was going through a messy divorce.

'Here,' he said, tossing Baxter a large, shiny red apple. 'It'll keep the doctor away - not sure about lawyers.' Baxter caught it one-handed.

'Thanks boss, you're the best,' he said, whilst

simultaneously holding the apple and stirring sugar in his coffee. He carried his brew over to the sofa and sank down low into the old foam cushions. Resting the mug on his knee, he shut his eyes and took in the unusual quietness. The loud ringing sound of the nearby telephone jolted him from his mini-nap. He gazed over at Kimberly, the shapely blonde PE teacher, as she answered it. She looked towards him and then covered the receiver with her free hand.

'It's for you, Nat,' she whispered. He rose slowly from the sofa and carried his warm coffee over to her.

'Thanks, Kimberly,' he said, as she passed him the handset.

'Hello,' said Nat, watching Kimberly saunter away.

'Mr. Baxter, this is Aaron Branson from *Branson & Jones Family Lawyers*. How are you?' Nathan's shoulders slumped, and he exhaled whatever energy he had left inside of him.

'Holding up as best I can, considering the circumstances,' he answered.

'That's great,' replied Branson, his voice emotionless and flat. 'Look, we're making good progress with your case and are meeting with Mrs. Baxter and her lawyer next week to finalise things. However, we note that you have an outstanding amount of $275 and are wondering if you can make payment on that, please.' Nathan closed his eyes, moved the phone away from his ear, rolled his head back, and sighed. He could sense that Kimberly was watching him.

'Sure,' he replied, wondering how on earth he was going to find such a large sum of money. 'Give me the payment details, and I'll send you a cheque.'

'Erm, the last one you sent us bounced, Mr. Baxter,' said the lawyer.

'Well, this one won't,' assured Nat, taking a blue biro from his pocket and once again asking for the details. He listened as Aaron Branson gave him the payment instructions, scrawling them on an open newspaper adjacent the phone. 'I'll see that it gets posted on Monday, and my ex-wife's name is Johanssen, not Baxter,' he said sarcastically. 'We're no longer married.'

'Is everything OK, Nat?' asked Kimberly as he hung up the phone.

'Good days and bad days, Miss Kimberly, and there's plenty of bad ones in my world at the moment,' he replied. She gave him a warm smile and placed her hand on his shoulder.

'Sometimes the waters of life are rough, but *you* are the master of your own ship,' she said. 'At least, I *think* that's how the phrase goes.' She giggled, and they both burst into laughter.

'Thanks Kimberly,' he said, holding up his now cold coffee mug and toasting her. He twirled the biro in his fingers and rubbed his eyes. Nat glanced back down at the payment details he'd written on the newspaper, when a job advert in bold font at the base of the page grabbed his attention. He scooped up the newspaper, quickly bringing it closer to his face.

It stated:

Music Teacher Wanted, immediate start, preferably skilled in piano or guitar. Good pay and working conditions, only qualified teachers need apply. Clare High School. Telephone: 851-5412.

Baxter was lost in thought and re-read the job advertisement.

'Clare, that's down on the south coast,' he mused.

'You look like you've seen a ghost,' uttered Kimberly.

'Not a ghost, but it is possible I'm looking into the future,' he replied before circling the ad. 'Captain Baxter. Master of his own ship,' he added, saluting Kimberly with a cheeky grin.

The afternoon's final two classes were uneventful, and the negativity was beginning to creep back up on him. He was also starting to talk himself out of applying for the job in Clare.

I've got a good job here, he thought. *I like my colleagues, and I also want to be close to Hanna.* He waited in line for his homeward-bound bus with a couple of other teachers and a handful of students - stragglers mostly, who had either missed their bus due to detention or were engaged in extra study. *Opposite ends of the 'student focus spectrum' now on display in the bus shelter. Screening daily at 4:45PM,* mused Nat. That creative brain of Baxter's was kicking into gear late in the day. He loved words and as a music fan, paid special attention to the lyrics. *Aaron Branson held me to ransom* he thought, humming a quiet melody. *I should put those lyrics into a song.*

Feeling tired and blue, he dragged himself off the bus and headed for the grocery store. He exited a short time later, armed with a TV dinner, a six-pack of Ashton Ale, and a small can of pilchards. As he entered his rental property, he noticed Checkers sunning herself in the front window, basking in the final rays of sunshine. Upon seeing Nathan, the cat sat up and stretched, arching her back after a long nap. After taking a bath, he walked into the kitchen and plugged in the electric can opener. Checkers reached up towards the kitchen bench top. She walked in between and around her owner's legs, affectionately rubbing her head against them. Nat manoeuvred the can around, then carefully flicked open the lid.

'Y'know, Check, it *was* impressive that we landed on the moon, there's no doubt about that, but I reckon the invention of the electric can opener is a far greater achievement,' he said, tapping the top of the machine with his finger…'and one giant leap for the feline-kind too.' The cat meowed hungrily as Baxter piled the small fish pieces into her bowl.

He grabbed a can of beer and headed for the lounge room. This routine had remained unchanged for several weeks now…work, home, drink, work, home, drink. He powered up the Hi-Fi and made his way, yet again, to *461 Ocean Boulevard.*

'My only two friends are alcohol and rock 'n' roll,' he mused. 'Oh, and you too, of course, Checkers.'

The next morning, he was woken early by Checkers wanting to go outside. He walked to the bathroom, gulped down two aspirin, then splashed water on his face in an attempt to keep the seedy feeling at bay. He got dressed, slid yesterday's newspaper ad into his back pocket and left for work early, hoping to put the extra time to good use. Missing his daughter and needing to hear the sound of her voice, Nat stepped into the telephone booth near his bus stop, deposited a coin and called his former home number. He listened as the connection was made. The repeated ringing sound made his heart thump a little and an uneasy feeling came over him, which he pushed away with a deep breath.

'Hello,' said Amber in her thick Swedish accent.

'Hi, it's me, Nat. I was just calling to wish Hanna a happy day at schoo'…..click. She'd hung up on him, and the silence on his end of the line was deafening. He pulled the handset away from his ear and stared into the mouthpiece in disbelief. The traffic whizzed by him on the adjacent four-lane road, but he could hear none of it. He felt his grip on the telephone grow tighter and he screamed in anger. He sensed that those in the bus shelter would be watching him but he didn't care. Nat closed his eyes and replaced the handset on the cradle. He stood motionless, staring blankly at the rotary dial on the telephone. He looked down at the weeds growing around the base of the telephone booth and then focused his gaze back on the dial. A quick surge of defiance ran through him. Baxter reached into his pocket and unfolded the page from the previous day's newspaper. He inserted another coin and dialled the telephone number for Clare High School.

| 2 |

The Astoria-Blue

How Nathan found himself living on Sweden's west coast in the summer of 1969 is a tale of opportunity, good fortune, and finally, fate. After the demise of Nathan and The Night-hawks in early '68, he attempted a solo career which never really got off the ground. He'd learned a lot in the two years with his own band and thought that some solo acoustic gigs could possibly lead to a recording contract. But gigs were hard to come by for an unknown kid whose only claim to fame was a suburban 'battle of the bands' win and the ensuing 7" release. So to pay the rent (and other bills), Nat took on a grimy factory job at a ship chandler, working alongside men old enough to be his grandfather - a couple of 'em had even fought in the Second World War. They were tough men too, who'd work hard, and then drink hard after knock-off at the local pub. Still, working in that warehouse did have its advantages. The ship chandler's major client was ship-ping giant J.T Archer & Wright, and Baxter's workplace was located directly across the road from a music store. He didn't keep track of his expenditures, but Baxter regularly handed over much of his pay packet for guitar strings, plectrums, and even a harmonica in that tiny little haven. He also took out a lay-by on one of the first effects pedals he'd seen. Sure, it was expensive, but ever since he'd heard those distorted tones which Keith Richards had created on 'Satisfaction,' he was intrigued. However, over time, intrigue had morphed into obsession, courtesy of Hendrix's 'Foxy Lady' and 'White Room' by Cream. By the late 1960s, the rock 'n' roll sound was a constantly evolving machine and a vehicle that Baxter wanted to ride. No, he didn't have the god-like guitar-playing ability of guys like Clapton and Jimi, but that didn't matter. Because he had a dream, and whenever he plugged into his second-hand VOX AC-30, that dream became a reality.

J.T. Archer & Wright operated a popular cruise on *The Astoria-Blue*, which would finish its six-week ocean journey at Southampton docks in the south of England. Baxter became aware of this while spying a promotional poster in the boss's office, late in the year.

'She's a beauty, isn't she?' said Mr. Donaldson, noticing Nat gazing over the glossy poster of the large passenger ship.

'Yes, sir, she certainly is,' replied Baxter.

'My wife and I went on *The Astoria-Blue* two summers ago and had a great time,' said Mr. Donaldson. 'There was a casino, great food too, and tons of booze as well. But it's not a 'booze cruise'. They also had a dance floor, and there was even a band on board too. Have you ever played mini golf, Baxter? Because on that ship, you can,' he laughed and proceeded to putt an imaginary ball.

'No, Sir, I haven't,' answered Nathan, his eyes wide after hearing that a band had performed on the ship. 'That'd be a cool gig, playing music on a cruise.'

'You play guitar, don't you, Baxter? One of the secretaries mentioned it.'

'Yeah, I do. Music's my life,' replied Nat.

'Hmmm,' pondered his boss whilst rubbing his chin. 'Y'know, next week I need to send a telegram to J.T. in London. I can enquire about it on your behalf and ask if there's any band vacancies available.'

'Far out, would you? That'd be great!' exclaimed Baxter enthusiastically, shaking Mr. Donaldson's hand in gratitude. Several days passed, and Nathan had pretty much forgotten their conversation - that is, until his boss called him back into his office with some exciting news. The young guitarist was in luck, as J.T. Archer & Wright currently had two vacant band positions for an upcoming Southampton-bound cruise - a guitarist and a drummer! After receiving a glowing reference from Mr. Donaldson, Nathan landed an audition on *The Astoria-Blue* when she was due to dock in mid-January. He was elated and confident he'd get the gig too. It just felt right. By the time of the audition, Nathan had been practising so much that the calluses on his fretting hand were as hard as granite, and his fingers felt more flexible than they'd ever been.

So, on a drizzly Wednesday evening in late January, Baxter arrived at the wharf clutching a guitar case, which held his beloved '59 Gibson Les Paul. On his back was an

Ovation balladeer acoustic guitar. He'd picked up the Gibson at a pawn shop when he was fifteen for $57 - most of which he'd borrowed from his Dad. He was initially attracted to the guitar because of its cherry-red, sunburst finish, but after playing it, loved the feel of the instrument. Baxter had yet to taste true romance, but knew he was in love with that guitar. After locating the cruise director, Nat was led into an audition room on the ship. There, he was introduced to a tall man clutching a bass guitar, who greeted him with a friendly smile. He had blonde, collar-length hair, and a walrus moustache which concealed his top lip. His name was Edvard Håkansson - born in Sweden, bass player, back-up vocalist, and unofficial band leader.

'Call me Ed,' he said.

'Only if you call me Nat,' replied Baxter with a grin. Edvard introduced Nathan to Dieter - the lead singer, and to a chubby drummer named Digby, who'd been chosen to fill the drum position earlier that afternoon. After jamming on 'Glad All Over' by the Dave Clark Five, they then performed a raucous take of '(I'm Not Your) Steppin' Stone' - a song made famous by The Monkees a couple of years earlier. They glanced approvingly at one another and nodded in silence - it was obvious there was some chemistry among the four players.

Exactly ten days later, Nathan had quit his job at the factory, obtained a passport, sold off some of his records for extra cash, and was waving farewell to his parents as *The Astoria-Blue* sailed out of the harbour. With some sadness, his Mum and Dad stood close together, waving back at their only child. It was Saturday, the first of February. Nat stood on the upper deck, strumming his guitar, while watching his folks fade into the distance.

'Rabbit, Rabbit Rabbit,' he mused, shutting his eyes tight. He then laughed aloud, remembering that this old, superstitious, good-luck phrase was meant to be uttered immediately upon waking on the first day of a new month. *Whatever* he thought, *it's gonna be a great month,* and then started strumming the chords to Jefferson Airplane's 'White Rabbit'. He walked back to his cabin, doing his best Grace Slick impersonation, garnering cheers and applause from several merry passengers.

The six-week cruise to the south of England was a great experience for Nathan, who'd never left his homeland. The gig with the band involved playing three sets per day, with Sundays off. Their repertoire was mostly Top 40 covers or familiar radio hits. They affectionately dubbed themselves The Astoria Blues Band and, on quiet nights, would sometimes break free from their restricted set-list and crank stuff by Cream, Elmore James or John Lee Hooker.

The thrill of being out at sea on a cruise liner, while getting paid to do something he loved, never wore off, and it was something Baxter found very appealing. Sure, the sunsets were amazing, but earning money while playing guitar? Man, that was the best - even if playing someone else's songs was not his desire, it was not forever. During their time together on the cruise, Nat and Ed formed a strong friendship, bonding over their mutual love of guys like Clapton, John Mayall, Hendrix and George Harrison. Many late nights were spent in the bar, chatting with girls or drunkenly debating recent album releases.

When *The Astoria-Blue* docked at Southampton in mid-March, Baxter bid farewell to the crew. Although he'd never suffered from sea-sickness during his time on the ship, he was nevertheless relieved to be back on dry land. He'd planned to do some travelling around England, maybe even take a ferry over to France if his money held out. After six weeks of non-stop playing, he also felt he had the chops to possibly join a band and planned to check out the 'musicians wanted' ads once he was settled in London.

As Nathan and Edvard lugged their gear to the bus station in Southampton, they saw a small crowd of people, including several photographers, a short distance away and decided to investigate. There was a couple with long dark hair standing together, dressed in white and holding hands. The lady was small and wore large sunglasses, while the bearded man wore round, wire-framed 'granny' glasses.

'Oh my god!' exclaimed Baxter, recognising who they were. 'That's John Lennon and Yoko Ono!'

'So it is!' replied Ed. 'But why on earth are they *here* in Southampton?'

'Konnichiwa, Yoko-san,' yelled Edvard. Baxter looked at him in surprise, unaware that his bass-playing pal spoke some Japanese. 'I've picked up a few phrases on past cruises,' he shrugged. Yoko looked over, smiled, and bowed a little.

'Hello, fellas,' said John, noticing the guitar cases Nat and Ed were carrying.

'Hey John, I dig 'Yer Blues', it's gear,' shouted Baxter,

name-checking one of his choice cuts from the Beatles' *White Album*, which they released the previous year.

'Well right on, brother,' replied Lennon in his thick Liverpudlian accent, whilst giving Nathan the thumbs-up. A swarm of photographers, press, and police then followed the famous couple as they made their way to a nearby office building. Nat and Ed stood there grinning, shaking their heads in disbelief.

'Far out,' uttered Nat. 'I gotta send a postcard back home and tell my folks I spoke to John Lennon! They'll never believe me!' he added. The two friends then checked-in their luggage and bought coffee, before boarding a coach bound for London.

'Give me a call if you make it to Sweden,' said Edvard after their bus arrived at London's Victoria Station.

'Thanks, Ed, I might just do that,' replied Baxter, giving him an arm-wrestle-style handshake.

Nathan made his way to the southeastern borough of Bromley and checked into a guesthouse operated by a lady in her 70s. Although it was mid-March, and winter had officially passed, London was experiencing a cold snap, and snow covered much of the capital. *I'd rather be back on the cruise,* he thought, rubbing his cold hands while surveying the snow-covered road from his bedroom window. The next morning, he awoke late and descended the stairs of the guesthouse, hungrily seeking the breakfast area.

'*It's located adjacent to the utility room,*' the old lady had told him when he checked in.

What the hell's a utility room? he pondered.

Baxter followed the aroma of fried bacon, mushrooms, baked beans, eggs, sausages, and toast and came upon a small room with three or four neatly set tables. He could hear the low rumble of a clothes dryer nearby and figured that the laundry area was the utility room. Nathan devoured his English breakfast while another guest, Mr. Singh, chatted about his tedious job as a bank clerk. He was so animated, that talking while eating cornflakes simultaneously created quite a mess. Nat watched as the milk trickled down Mr. Singh's beard, and he offered him a napkin.

'If you don't like it, why don't you just quit and find something else?' suggested Nat, offering a solution to his breakfast buddy's grievances.

'One day, Mr. Nathan, I hope to be the bank manager, so I must never give up.'
Baxter listened, then washed down a piece of toast smeared in marmalade with a mouthful of orange juice.

'That's cool, brother. Chase down your dream,' he said.

'Are you a musician?' asked Mr. Singh. Baxter nodded. 'I could tell because of the hair and the jacket.

'I play guitar,' added Nat, pretending to run his fingers along an imaginary fretboard.
Mr. Singh stood, placed his chair under the table, and extended his hand to Nathan.

'If you can play the guitar, then you can play the sitar - an incredible instrument. Now that is a dream to chase,' he said smiling. Baxter, aware of the great sitar player Ravi Shankar via his connection to The Beatles, smiled back at him.

With a nearly full stomach, Baxter squeezed in a cup

of tea, then went back to his room to snooze. After watching the news headlines, followed by a dull program about farming in Yorkshire, Baxter switched the TV off then made his way to the High Street. He bought a copy of the *New Musical Express* and sat down with a pint of Guinness at a pub named *The Scape Goat*. Nat scanned over the gig guide in search of groups he was familiar with.

'Hey man, you a musician?' asked a voice. Baxter turned around and saw a skinny man with gaunt cheeks. He was wearing a loose purple shirt with dirty blue jeans and had long, greasy brown hair parted in the centre. A thin leather headband kept the hair out of his eyes.

'Yes brother, I am,' replied Nat with a smile. 'I play guitar. You want a pint?' he asked the stranger, who nodded and then pulled up a stool. 'I've just been gigging on a cruise ship,' said Nat. 'It's nice to have a beer without swaying. Although, that may come later,' he chuckled, holding up his pint and slowly sipping the dark stout. Nat wiped the remnants of the foamy head from his lips with his sleeve before continuing. 'Do you know any good bands playing around town?' The wiry hippie shut his eyes and dragged on a cigarette. He thought for a moment, then exhaled the smoke skyward.

'Yeah, there's an Irish band called Taste you should check out. Their guitar player is outta sight,' he said, holding out his glass and clinking it with Baxter's. 'I really dig the Grateful Dead, man, and that whole Frisco scene.....it's a trip.'

'I wrote a psychedelic song a few years ago called 'Vanilla Stars', commented Nathan.

'Groovy,' replied the hippie. 'Oh!' he blurted out, flailing his arms and nearly sending Baxter's pint over. 'Country Joe and the Fish! Cool group. They're playing at the Marquee, I think, on the 28th.'

'Country Joe and the Fish,' repeated Baxter. 'Thanks for the tip, brother.'
Nathan finished his pint and returned to the guesthouse after shopping for clothes on the High Street.

Any thoughts of joining a band were put on hold as he first wanted to explore some of the country. By the end of April, he'd been to Liverpool, Manchester, Birmingham, and as far north as Glasgow and Inverness in Scotland. But the travel costs were adding up and he was burning through the savings he'd earned on *The Astoria-Blue*. So he made the decision to travel to Sweden and hook up with Edvard - maybe he could even find a gig there?

Baxter did however make his way to the Marquee in Wardour Street on the 28th, but the hippie in the pub had his dates wrong. Country Joe and the Fish were in fact playing the following night. Nevertheless, Baxter spent that Friday evening in late March, taking in the powerful sounds of a new local group called Led Zeppelin. Impressed with what he'd seen, he went and purchased their self-titled debut record a few weeks later and shipped it back home. He also slipped a postcard inside the LP for his parents...

26th April, 1969: Hi Mum and Dad, I am writing to you on a partly cloudy day here in London. Things are going OK. Since my last postcard, which I sent from that island-stop on the cruise, I've been checking out the sights - well, mostly a lot of book and record shops along with some amazing music stores in an area called Soho. I visited Liverpool recently. No, I didn't see any Beatles, but I did, in fact, bump into John and Yoko on the day I arrived here - true story! I am departing the U.K. soon, bound for Gothenburg in Sweden. My ferry for the southern French city of Calais departs tomorrow. From there, I'll head to Antwerp, Hamburg, and Copenhagen. Then it's another ferry ride from Denmark to Sweden. Well, that's the plan for now! Edvard, (my fellow band member from the cruise) is from Gothenburg and invited me to visit. I have included his address on this postcard. Even though I'm a million miles from home, you are both in my thoughts (that sounds like a song lyric!) - I've been writing a lot recently. Miss you, Nat

PS - You can play this album if you wish, but it may be somewhat louder than your Seekers LPs!

Two days later, and with the sun nearly set, Baxter's train rolled into Gothenburg Central Station. Exhausted, he rubbed his eyes, stretched, and lugged his guitars and small bag onto the platform.

'Hej Nat!' hollered a loud voice. Baxter looked over the crowd of passengers to see Edvard grinning. The two friends hugged and slapped each other on the back. 'I see you've packed the most important things,' said Ed, pointing to Nat's guitar case, which housed the '59 Les Paul. Baxter laughed. 'Oh, this is my girlfriend, Brigitta,' he added, introducing Nat to the pretty blonde girl standing beside him.

'Hallå,' she said, smiling. Baxter noted that when she smiled, the dimples on her cheeks appeared, lighting up her face like a Christmas tree. Her long hair was tied back in a sleek ponytail, and she wore a red leather jacket over a white turtleneck sweater. With her diamond- blue eyes, Brigitta had the looks of a stereotypical Swedish girl, and Nat could already see Ed was smitten. They hauled Nat's guitars and bag into a taxi and drove to their apartment in the nearby suburb of Pärva. It was a leafy area lined with beech and maple trees, with several cafés, galleries, and book stores. Ed and Brigitta's apartment was located opposite a canal, and there was a bread shop adjacent to their apartment.

'You can smell freshly baked bread when you wake up; it's really wonderful,' said Brigitta, pointing to the small bakery. Baxter was hungry and smiled at the thought.

'Nat, there's also quite a few bars and kafés, or I should say - cafés, around here that have live music. So, I'm hoping you and I might get some gigs happening,' added Ed, as they exited the taxi.

'Fab, that's music to my ears, brother!'

Nat rested his guitar case down on the road, then handed some krona to his friend to help cover the cost of the fare. *This is a lovely area* he thought, as the cab drove away. As he reached for the handle on his case, Brigitta shrieked and pointed at him.

'Don't move, look where you're standing, don't move!' she cried out. Baxter looked puzzled and frowned. 'Here in Sweden, there is a superstition that if you step on a 'K' manhole cover, you'll have good luck and find love!' she said excitedly. Nat looked down at his feet to see that he had indeed plonked his guitar case on a manhole cover and was standing on one marked with the letter 'K'. Brigitta was grinning and continued. 'We avoid the manhole covers with the letter 'A' as they bring bad luck. But standing on the 'K' cover will bring you love because 'K' stands for kärlek, which means 'love'.

'It actually stands for *kulvertnedgång*. *Kulvert* is a sort of tunnel and *nedgång* means way down. So, way down to the tunnel,' said Ed, shaking his head. 'I've tried explaining to Brigitta that this is just an urban myth, but….' he exhaled and held out his hands.

'What does the 'A' stand for?' queried Nathan.

'*Avlopp*,' replied Ed, 'which in English means 'sewage.' Appropriate too, as it sums up what most of these superstitions are all about.'

'It's true,' argued Brigitta. 'Before I found you, Edvard, I stood on a 'K' cover one cold December evening. Light snow was falling, and I wished that true love would find me.'
Ed gave his girlfriend a sympathetic smile and kissed her on the forehead.

'C'mon, let's go inside,' he said, collecting Baxter's luggage. 'It's really great to see you again brother.'

They spent the evening listening to records and drinking wine before going to bed. Nat stretched out on the sofa and buried his head in a soft pillow. Within minutes, courtesy of the wine and accompanied by exhaustion, he was sound asleep.

| 3 |

Kärlek

Brigitta was right about waking to the smell of bread; only, the next morning, it was coming from *their* kitchen and not the adjacent bakery. She was cutting a hot loaf of limpa bread she'd just purchased into thick slices, and the scent of rye filled the apartment. Nat sat up and yawned, then glanced at his wrist watch - it was a quarter past ten. Before she made her way to a nearby clothing store where she worked, Brigitta made coffee and scrambled eggs to accompany the limpa bread. Then she, Nathan, and Ed ate on the balcony, enjoying the mid-morning sunshine. As she was checking herself in the mirror, Brigitta noticed Nat's passport, along with his wallet, and a guitar plectrum resting on the coffee table. Curious, as she'd never seen one, she opened up and inspected the official-looking document.

'Oh my God!' she shrieked, attracting the attention of both lads. 'You were born on the same day as Paul McCartney!' Nathan looked over at Brigitta, who was pointing at the information page of the booklet. '18th of June!' she added.

'Right on!' said Baxter, unaware but delighted to learn that he shared a birthday with Beatle Paul.

'That's heavy,' chimed Ed. 'Paul was eight years old when you were born.'

Nathan nodded.

After Brigitta left for work, Baxter and Edvard sat around drinking beer and playing Beatles tunes on their acoustic guitars. Although they hadn't played together since the cruise, the chemistry between the two was instant. First song they tackled was a faithful rendition of 'I'll Follow The Sun,' which Baxter unexpectedly cut-short, eager to share a story.

'Hey Ed, I think Paul wrote that one when he was still living at his childhood home on Forthlin Road. I even checked out the house when I recently travelled through Liverpool.'

'Get outta here!' replied Ed, chuckling at his friend's crazy antics.

'True,' confirmed Nat, taking a swig of beer.

'But I read that they moved out ages ago?' queried Ed.

'So did I, but I knocked on the door anyway. Some lady answered and confirmed that they sold up some time ago. She kindly invited me in for a cup of tea, but I declined.'

Edvard shook his head in amazement and proposed a toast in honor of Nat's fandom. The duo then resumed their band practice in earnest and the mood was upbeat. When they harmonised on the song 'I'll Be Back,' they even attracted a couple of onlookers from outside, who peered up at the balcony and clapped. Edvard waved at them and bowed.

'Let's do 'And I Love Her' from *A Hard Day's Night*, it's Brigitta's favourite Beatles song,' said Ed, settling himself into his orange Sacco chair. When they'd finished the song, he smiled over at Baxter in admiration. 'It's like McCartney's in the room my friend; your pitch is perfect on that number.'

'Thanks brother,' said Nat. 'Maybe it's an 18th of June thing.'

'Y'know, Brigitta *really* digs the Beatles and is envious that we bumped into John and Yoko. She saw the Fab Four play in Stockholm back in '64. She was one of those screaming teenage girls,' laughed Ed.

'Groovy,' replied Nat, resting his guitar on a stand. He took a swig from his beer bottle, then flicked through Edvard's record collection, selecting the Beatles' *White Album*. He dropped the needle on 'While My Guitar Gently Weeps' and stood in awe at the sounds coming through the speakers. 'I heard Eric Clapton plays on this number - well, it's a rumour, I guess. A roadie I was chatting with at the Marquee in London told me.'

Ed spat out some beer in shock.

'No way! That's not true. That's *Harrison* playing - I can tell,' he argued. '*..and* the Beatles are a tight unit, man. They don't allow just anyone to enter the studio. It's their inner sanctum. Only the four.... and producer George Martin too, of course.'

'Ed, I'm just telling you what I was told, and to my ears, that sounds like Clapton's licks,' reasoned Nat. 'I think it's true, and it makes sense - and Clapton is not just *anyone*. Plus, he and George Harrison have been friends for years - since the Yardbirds did some shows with the Beatles.' Ed shook his head in disagreement, took another swig, and turned up the volume on the stereo.

'I read in the newspaper that Clapton is currently in a hot new group called Blind Faith.'

'Wow! That's cool,' replied Nat.

'Yeah, he's brought Ginger Baker with him from Cream, and there's a couple of cats from Traffic in there as well. They've got an album coming out soon too,' explained Ed. He and Nathan clinked their beer bottles with delight before heading to the refrigerator for a refill. As there was no more beer, they exited the apartment and spent the afternoon and early evening in a local bar named The Avondet. Run by a middle-aged Swiss beatnik, The Avondet was popular with university students and avant-garde musicians. Edvard and Brigitta had previously visited the bar for a poetry reading. Before staggering back to the apartment, Ed and Nat informed the owner that they were guitarists seeking work. Upon learning that they had recently been playing on a cruise liner, they were hired on the spot.

The gigs at The Avondet turned out to be a lot of fun, even if Nathan wasn't too keen on the Håkansson and Baxter billing which the bar owner had insisted on. However, the money was OK, and, importantly for Nat, most of the punters were really into the music and would give their full attention to him and Ed. Nothing made him happier.

Most of Nat's earnings went to Ed and Brigitta to cover his board and lodgings, but whatever krona he had left over he'd spend on books, beer, and records. Some days he'd spend hours alone in the leafy parks or cafés, writing in his journal or working on song ideas. A couple of these songs found their way into the live set at The Avondet, interspersed with obscure covers.

One Sunday evening in late May, Nat struck up a conversation with a music journalist from Stockholm who'd been impressed with what he'd heard of Håkansson and Baxter.

'I dig the way you blow harp, man, on that Cream cover, 'Spoonful'', he said.

'Thanks brother,' replied Nat. 'It's actually a number penned by Willie Dixon, but Howlin' Wolf cut it before the Cream did. Willie also wrote 'Little Red Rooster' which the Stones later recorded.' The journalist nodded his head, impressed with Nat's music knowledge. He leaned closer and whispered.

'I can tell you are a fan of Clapton, so let me give you a scoop,' whispered the visitor from Stockholm, leaning in close. He now had Nathan's full attention who nodded his head and listened intently. 'His new group, Blind Faith, are performing in Gothenburg next month. They're doing a few concerts in Scandinavia before an American tour, but I *can* confirm they're playing Stockholm and then here, at the nearby Liseberg, two days later. It will be announced in the music press the day after tomorrow.'

Baxter was ecstatic and rushed over to share the news with Ed, who was busy packing up their gear. They rounded out the evening by downing a few shots of whiskey in another bar with their new friend from Stockholm. At around two in the morning, they left the bar and then parted company.

'Hey, thanks again f..f..for the Blind Faif news,' slurred Nathan, slapping the drunk journalist on the back. 'Ed, Ed, how can I say thankyou?' he asked. Edvard stood with his hands in his pockets and laughed.

'It's tack, Nat. Tack is the word,' said Ed before belching.

'Gotcha. Tack, brother, tack, tack,' shouted Nat to the Stockholmer as he walked away. He turned and gave a 'you're welcome'-type wave. 'Blind Faith. Man, that's gonna be a gas,' garbled Nat before turning to Ed. 'I'm pretty blind now, brother Edwardo,' he laughed. The two friends gathered their guitar cases and staggered back to the apartment.

While Brigitta worked, Edvard and Nathan nursed large hangovers, surfacing late in the afternoon. Sure enough, in the following day's newspaper (just as the journalist had stated), Ed read details of the upcoming Blind Faith concert in Gothenburg. By the time the weekend rolled around, he had secured tickets for himself, Brigitta, and Baxter!

Nathan spent the first couple of weeks in June immersed in his songwriting, while also trying to learn some Swedish phrases. He wasn't sure how long he was going to remain in Gothenburg, but with the Håkansson and Baxter gigs at The Avondet starting to pull a regular crowd, he wanted to be able to communicate with punters from the stage. He also knew that language was a key that could open many doors. The new musical duo had even been attempting to write a song combining English and Swedish lyrics.

Wednesday, the 18th of June 1969 was the date of the Blind Faith concert. It also happened to be Baxter's birthday!

He eased into the day slowly, surfacing around midday. He made coffee, then sat on the balcony with his guitar and notebook. Compared to other cities, the summer heat of Gothenburg was mild, which Nathan, not a fan of hot weather, found appealing. A light breeze touched the base of the curtain which separated the living room from the balcony. The sombre sounds of a violinist, busking in the nearby marketplace filled the air. Nathan lowered his notebook, took a sip of coffee, and listened.

'Why does the violin make people feel so goddamn melancholy?' he mused. *I guess happiness and sadness walk hand in hand - sometimes apart, but never far from each other.*

He nodded and jotted down that phrase before closing his eyes. Nat nestled the acoustic guitar comfortably on his knee and began picking out the notes to Simon & Garfunkel's 'The Sound of Silence'. Life was good.

Edvard and Brigitta returned home around 5:30PM. For his birthday, they presented Nat with LPs by local artists, such as The Hootenanny Singers and The Hep Stars. He was delighted.

After a light meal, the three friends made their way to the concert hall which was located within the nearby Liseberg Amusement Park. They walked through the park, passing a large roller coaster, ferris wheel, dodgem cars, and an assortment of other rides and attractions.

'That looks scary,' said Brigitta, pointing at the people in the car as it sped along the tracks of the wooden roller coaster. But Baxter's attention was elsewhere, drawn in by the alluring lights of some pinball machines located in a nearby arcade hall.

'I'll catch up with you guys later,' he said. Ed looked at his friend and smiled, aware of Nat's love of the silver ball.

'Go get a high score, brother. We'll see you inside.'

Baxter bought a beer, rested it on a nearby table, and deposited a coin into the machine. There was something mesmerising about pinball that made Nathan feel totally at peace. He'd been playing since his teenage years, and that, along with rock 'n' roll, was all he really needed to reach a level of total contentment. He took a large gulp of lager, then pulled the plunger back, watching the silver ball shoot to the top of the board and pass through the spinners. Pushing his weight on the corners of the front cabinet, Baxter did his best to control the ball as it ricocheted off the bumpers. His hand-eye coordination was fast and was one of the skills that contributed to his pinball prowess. He also just really dug it. He loved the escape - and it was a love affair that would stay with him for many, many years.

After half an hour or so, Nat lost his final ball, so finished his beer and made his way to the concert hall, leaving behind a couple of free games for the next player to enjoy. As he entered the hall, the amplified sound of the opening act, Babylon, permeated through the air, combined with the strong odour of grass. Baxter pulled his ticket from his back pocket and studied it. *Bänk 7, Plats 4.* He walked over to the bar and ordered three beers, then pointed to his ticket as the barmaid filled the glasses.

'Hej, what do these words mean in English?' he

shouted. The barmaid looked at his ticket and placed a beer down on the bar.

'*Bänk is a bench, y'know like a seat, and Plats is 'place,*' she replied loudly. Nat nodded his appreciation and thanked her. Balancing the three beers, Baxter located his seat, then handed a beer to both Edvard and Brigitta.

'These cats are cool,' shouted Edvard, motioning to the band on stage. 'But I think Håkansson and Baxter would give 'em a run for their money,' he added. Ed and Baxter raised their glasses in agreement. After one further song, Babylon finished their set and the house lights came on. Many of the concert-goers raced off to the bar, the toilets, or sat around chatting. The Blind Faith concert had been highly antici-pated, and Baxter stood with his eyes shut, absorbing the atmosphere.

'Ursäkta mig, är det här plats nummer 3?' said a voice to his left.

Nathan looked over and in an instant felt his heart ex-plode. She was wearing a black and white houndstooth skirt, white gogo boots and a matching, white, sleeveless, turtle-neck top. She looked gorgeous and Baxter gave her a smile. Although his Swedish was minimal, he knew the girl, who looked about twenty years old, was asking if her seat was number 3.

'Ja det är det,' he replied, indicating she did have the correct seat. He let out a sigh, grateful that his recent study of Swedish phrases had been useful.

'Tack,' she replied, before turning to a friend she was with. Both girls giggled and sat down.

'My name's Nathan,' said Baxter with a smile. He couldn't take his eyes off her.

'I'm Amber,' she replied, 'Are you from Gothenburg?'

'No, I'm just visiting,' said Nat.

'You look like you're in a band,' said Amber, noting Baxter's blue jeans and black leather jacket.

'I play guitar. This is my friend and bandmate, Edvard,' replied Nat, motioning to Ed. 'And this is his girlfriend, Brigitta.' The two girls smiled at each other. Amber then turned to her left and introduced her friend, Karita, to Nat and his friends.

'Karita is a huge music fan and loves rock 'n' roll. She had an extra ticket, which is why I'm here.'

'I saw Jimi Hendrix here a couple of years ago, and also saw Cream live in concert as well. They were outta sight,' said Karita proudly. Baxter was impressed and raised his beer.

'I'd love to see Hendrix live. He and Clapton are gods. *Electric Ladyland,* man, what an album, what an album!' enthused Nat. Karita nodded her agreement.

'Well, I'm glad I came here tonight,' said Amber with a warm smile. She stared at Nathan for a long time and softly touched his arm.

'So am I,' he replied, returning Amber's stare. She moved her hand to his and reached for the beer glass.

'May I?' she asked, keen for a sip. Nat nodded and released the glass. 'Skål,' she said, lifting the beer to her lips. She took a large gulp before handing it back to Baxter.

'Cheers,' he said before taking a swig himself, never once taking his eyes off her. The house lights dimmed, and a couple of thousand enthusiastic music fans focused their eyes on the stage. With minimal fanfare, Blind Faith took to the stage and kicked off with a forceful take of 'Well All Right'. Buddy Holly may've penned it a decade or so earlier, but Clapton and Co. had taken the song to another level. Some years later, in Nat's opinion, Santana would elevate the tune to even greater heights. The band sounded fantastic and Baxter was enjoying every minute of it.

'Clapton is God,' Edvard yelled in his friend's ear. Nathan clasped his hands, bowed his head, and pretended to pray.

'In the presence of the Lord, my friend, in the presence of the Lord.' They both laughed. Fourth song into the set was a faithful rendition of the Stones' 'Under My Thumb'. Nat looked over at Amber, grabbed her hands, and started dancing. Brigitta smiled and then she and Ed began grooving as well. Nathan steered his way to the aisle where there was more room.

From this vantage point he noticed a couple of denim-clad fans with a reel to reel tape recorder hidden under their seats. One of the guys copped Baxter looking at him and nodded.

'Right on!' shouted Nat, giving the bootlegger the thumbs-up. At the end of the song, the audience were on their feet clapping loudly. Baxter and Amber remained standing in the aisle, and slow-danced to the next song, 'Can't Find My Way Home'. Listening to Clapton's guitar work wrap itself around Steve Winwood's vocals while holding Amber close to him, was a moment in time that Nathan would carry with him forever.

Nathan and Edvard quickly went to the bar and returned with drinks for everyone.

'How are you enjoying the concert?' Baxter asked Karita while handing her a beer.

'Fantastiskt!' she replied in a heavy Swedish accent. 'I cannot wait to buy their album.' Nat smiled in agreement and returned to his seat.

If these songs are a preview of the forthcoming album, then it's gonna be one helluva record, thought Nat.

The Blind Faith set came to an end all too soon, and the return of the house lights signalled the end of the concert.

'Man, that was cool!' said Ed, tapping Baxter on the shoulder.

'I agree, brother. The band was tight and in top form,' he replied.

'Hey, why don't we all go for a drink?' suggested Ed.

'I can't,' replied Karita. 'I have to work early tomorrow morning, but thanks anyway.'

'No sweat,' said Ed. 'Nat? Post-gig drink? The Avondet?'

'Man, I'm gonna pass too. Amber and I are going to take a walk around the Park. But I'll see you both back home later on.' Amber was blushing a little before she spoke.

'A walk sounds like a wonderful idea, Nathan. I'd like that.' Brigitta grabbed Edvard's hand and tightened it, alerting him to the chemistry between Amber and Nat.

Edvard bellowed loudly through the chorus of 'Well Alright', as they all headed for the exit door. After saying their farewells, Baxter and Amber bought ice cream and strolled slowly around the Amusement Park. They sat close together on a bench in front of the Ferris wheel, which was illuminated with tiny blue and white butterfly lights. The sky was filled with what seemed like a thousand stars and a half-moon that sat high above. The Park was relatively quiet, except for a handful of concert-goers drinking noisily at a nearby bar.

Amber turned her head to face him.

'I have a feeling you're going to steal my heart,' she said.

Nathan looked lovingly at her and smiled.

'I have a feeling you're right,' he replied, leaning over to kiss her as a gentle breeze swept through the park. They both smiled and laughed.

'It's getting chilly, and it's also time I said goodnight,' said Amber, getting to her feet. She wrote her telephone number on the back of her concert ticket and handed it to Nathan.

Baxter then removed his leather jacket, placing it over Amber's shoulders as they walked to the taxi rank.

'Thankyou for a wonderful evening,' she said, before kissing him goodbye.

'You're beautiful,' replied Nat, hugging her tight. They gazed into each other's eyes one final time before he helped her into the rear of the vehicle. Baxter stood and waved farewell to Amber as the cab pulled out onto the road. She looked back at him through the window and smiled. Feelings of love and elation coursed through his body and he'd never felt so alive. This was by far the best night of his life! Blind Faith were incredible, Clapton lived up to his expectations, *and* he'd met Amber. Feeling buoyant, he thought about stopping at a telephone booth and making a long-distance call to his folks, but quickly changed his mind when remembering how expensive an international call could be. He decided to write them a postcard the next day instead.

Nathan started walking back to Ed and Brigitta's apartment, oblivious to the fact that Amber was still wearing his leather jacket.

Since the Blind Faith concert in June, Amber and Nat were virtually inseparable. He continued living with Edvard and Brigitta, both of whom welcomed Amber into their world. In July, the four friends gathered around the TV at The Avondet and watched astronauts Armstrong and Aldrin walk on the moon. It was a feat that blew Baxter's mind, though he wasn't entirely sure how he felt about it and whether visiting other planets was a high priority. He preferred the clear, blue skies to be filled with fresh air and birds rather than rockets and satellites.

'I guess it'd be pretty quiet up there,' he said. 'Floating all alone in a galactic egg - space solitude, man, the perfect place to write songs! Wait, with all that microgravity, would my guitar float away? And what about my plectrum? I'd have to glue it to my fingers.' Ed spat out his beer, and they all laughed loudly at Baxter's vivid imagination. Nat held out his hands to indicate his question was a serious one. Then, he broke into laughter as well.

When Blind Faith's debut album was released the following month, Nat and Edvard eagerly bought a copy and almost wore out the grooves! And it wasn't just the six songs contained on that black vinyl platter that resonated with

Baxter. In his mind, it was *because* of Blind Faith that he had found Amber! The days passed into weeks; the summer faded, and then Autumn turned cold. Nathan and Amber were deep in love.

He loved the cold weather, and the Christmas of 1969 was one of the happiest times in his life. Amber's family - the Johanssens, loved him like a son, and her younger sister Evelina adored him.

He spent Christmas Eve with the Johanssens, eating far too much Christmas ham (or julskinka as Evelina had politely corrected him), limpa bread, and too many glasses of glögg - the traditional, warm, spicy homemade liquor that provided quite a punch - pun intended. After they opened presents, Baxter sat in front of the open fire with his guitar, singing Christmas songs with Amber and her father. When everyone had gone to bed, he walked outside the house, surveyed the snow on the ground, and watched the Christmas lights as they swayed in the cold breeze. He downed the final remnants of a beer, hummed the chorus to The Beatles' 'A Day In The Life,' and looked skyward. He thought about his parents back home, and all that had happened since he went for that audition on *The Astoria-Blue*. A black cat scurried past, staring at Nat with its green eyes before disappearing down a drain. Nathan could see the bedside lamp still on in Amber's bedroom. He looked at the clear sky for one long and final time and smiled. He was happy, he was in love, he felt 'home'.

Amber and Nathan got engaged in the summer of 1970 and were married in early September. It was a week that

Baxter would never forget, as he and his best man, Edvard, went to see The Jimi Hendrix Experience one electrifying Tuesday evening at Liseberg. Several beers, along with too many shots of cinnamon-flavoured schnapps, helped to make the concert a memorable one.

'My last concert as a free man,' joked Nat, not realising at the time just how poignant his comment would turn out to be. Hendrix was phenomenal, and both Ed and Nat stood there, fully immersed, taking in every note - mesmerised by his god-like guitar playing. Baxter had long believed that rock 'n' roll was spiritual, so, aware they were witnessing something special, he joined his hands in a prayer-like gesture, as he had done at the Blind Faith show, and looked to the heavens while Jimi played the solo in 'Hey Joe'. The guitarist noticed Baxter mid-rock 'n' roll prayer. He pointed, smiled and acknowledged him with a nod. Baxter saluted, returned the smile, then he and Edvard hugged each other, celebrating the once-in-a-lifetime moment. It was a moment that would stay with Nat forever, as Hendrix would be found dead in London later that month.

The wedding was a traditional ceremony, held at a local church attended by family and friends. Amber looked stunning and wore a beautiful French Chantilly lace dress, embroidered with floral sequins. Her bridesmaid, Evelina, also looked pretty and cried throughout much of the ceremony. Later, the Johanssens held a large garden party to celebrate their daughter's wedding. Nathan wished his parents could be there to enjoy the celebration, but they sent a telegram offering their congratulations. His folks would be spending lots of time getting to know their new daughter-in-law, as she and Nathan had decided to depart Sweden and start their married life in Baxter's homeland. And so, in late 1970, Nathan and Amber Baxter bid a tearful farewell to family and friends at Torslanda airport. Nat checked in his two guitar cases and watched them disappear along the conveyor belt. They'd served him well and would continue to do so. As their Scandinavian Airlines flight was being refuelled for the long journey ahead, the well-wishers all gathered at the airport bar for a final farewell drink. Nathan downed two beers before the boarding call for Flight SA22 echoed over the PA, and the couple made their way to the boarding gate. He turned his head to see Ed and Brigitta waving from an upper level. Nat felt indebted to both of them. The two guitarists locked eyes and smiled.

'I'm gonna miss you, brother,' yelled Ed loudly.
Baxter nodded but had to look away as he felt tears welling up. He took a deep breath and exhaled, then headed to the gate with his arm around Amber.

| 4 |

Per Volar Sunata

With its white, sandy beaches, picturesque harbour, and small population, the sleepy coastal town of Clare seemed a world away from Gothenburg. Baxter stood on the creaking wharf with his hands in his pockets, watching the fishing boats as they bobbed up and down. The small blinking lights and the sound of the wind, flapping in their sails were somewhat comforting. A light, misty rain began to fall, and he pulled his hood up over his head.

Welcome to Clare, where the rain and ocean merge - stated the slogan on the roadside signs at both ends of town. *Seems accurate*, he mused, recalling the town slogan he'd seen, when driving into Clare earlier that afternoon. It was mid-Autumn, and Baxter had just arrived in town, after successfully applying for the teaching position at Clare High. After a turbulent few months, he wasn't really sure if he was making the right move. But he was going nuts at that rental home and had lost all enthusiasm for his teaching gig at South Fletcher High School. Nat desperately needed a change.

He hadn't eaten all day, and his grumbling stomach reminded him that it was dinner time. Before trekking back to his motel room, he stopped in at a burger joint named Nugget's for a meal. The place was empty apart from two teenage kids who sat in a booth by the window. Nat walked to the jukebox and hovered over it, checking the titles, before reaching into his pocket for change. He made his selection and listened as the first strains of 'All Along The Watchtower' by Jimi Hendrix roared from the speakers.

'Hello, old friend,' he said aloud to the ghost of Hendrix, as a smile formed on his face. The teenagers glanced over and nodded their approval. Baxter made his way to the counter and ordered a hamburger with the lot and large cola. He sauntered over to three flashing pinball machines lined up near the jukebox. He stopped at *The Six Million Dollar Man* machine, rested his cola on the ground, fed in a coin, and re-entered the zone of the silver ball - a place he knew well. Twenty five minutes later he had acquired the high score.

'Hey Mac, we're closing up soon,' yelled the cook from the kitchen. Baxter copped the hint, looked up, and nodded. He presumed it was the joint's owner, Nugget. Nat removed his fingers from the flippers, allowing the ball in play to roll into the drain area. The dumpy cook walked over to Nat, whilst wiping his hands on the front of a dirty apron. 'Sheesh Mac, you're pretty hot,' he said. 'That high score's been standing for about six months. You're, ahm…' he paused, searching for the right word. Nathan raised his cola bottle at the cook and grinned.

'Bionic?' he suggested, then exited the cafe with his food. The rain had stopped, so he strolled back to the wharf and noticed two seagulls grappling over some discarded french fries. Baxter stood still and watched small waves slap against a yacht's hull. He sighed and felt the sea breeze flow over him. He hadn't felt at peace like this in some time. This was nice.

Several yards away, he noticed what appeared to be quite a large oyster farm submerged in the water. Located nearby was an accompanying sign that read *Montgomery Oysters - where the world is yours*. Baxter laughed aloud at the failed play on words. *I wonder what English scholar came up with that?* he thought.

After a few more moments of solitude, he made his way back to the motel, stopping at a milk bar to grab some chocolate and chewing gum. He walked through the fly-strip blinds and exited the store, tearing off the end of the chocolate bar with his teeth. A flier in the store window grabbed his attention and he stopped to read it:

House for rent, 3 bedrooms, garage, small garden, close to beach. Pets ok. Phone: 851-1729.

'Man, this sounds ideal,' he said aloud, making note of the telephone number. 'I'll chase it up first thing tomorrow.'

After sleeping soundly, Baxter read the newspaper over coffee, showered and made plans to check out the rental property. He was due to start his teaching position later in the week and had allowed himself a few days to find somewhere to live and get settled. The house was located in Auger

Avenue and as the ad in the window had stated, it was indeed, close to the beach. In fact, it was only one street away, or an easy five-minute stroll. As soon as Nathan walked into the old weatherboard cottage, he loved it. It wasn't big, it wasn't modern, but it had a charm, a warmth, and a character that spoke to him. There was a cosy front porch that held an unloved velour sofa and matching wooden table.

'I apologise, I need to replace that,' said the owner, pointing to the furniture.

'There's no need,' replied Nat. 'It's perfect just the way it is. You mentioned in the ad that pets are allowed. I have a cat.'

'Yes, pets are fine,' confirmed the owner.

'Perfect,' said Nat, glancing over at the sofa and table. This was a place where he could write music and play guitar, a place to read, and ultimately, a place where he could find solace. He smiled and extended his hand. 'I'll take it.'

As the property was vacant, Nat made plans to move in as soon as possible. Having found a place to live so quickly had freed up his time, so he checked out of the motel and decided to head back to Fletcher that day to gather his belongings. He also needed to arrange a cat cage for Checkers and collect her from the elderly neighbour who'd been caring for her. After that, he had to sign some paperwork at the lawyer's office before collecting a farewell gift at South Fletcher High, which Terry, Kimberly, and other staff members had purchased for him. He ultimately gave up on searching for a cat cage and ended up just punching some air holes in a sturdy cardboard box instead. Checkers didn't seem to mind and slept most of the trip anyway.

One of the very first things Baxter did upon arriving at his new rental property was to brew some coffee and then hook up the Hi-Fi. *Candles In The Rain* and *Garden In The City,* two of his favourite Melanie albums, both shared lots of time on the turntable that afternoon and early evening. Her powerful voice soared throughout the rooms - the nearest thing to a blessing for his new house that he could wish for. He also plugged in the refrigerator, and shelved some milk and butter which he'd purchased on the drive down. He spread some of the butter onto Checkers' paws – an old superstition intended to help the cat settle into a new home. Apparently, the feline licks the butter, and therefore removes the scent and smell of its former surroundings. Nat didn't know whether this worked or not, but he put his scepticism to one side, as he'd seen his mother previously do it with their cat, Smokey. He refilled his coffee mug, lit an incense stick, then walked out to the porch.

'Now *this* is the life, isn't it, Checkers?' he said, nestling into the old sofa. His furry black and white companion meowed and then jumped up onto the sofa, settling in his lap. He took a sip of the strong coffee and shut his eyes. He could hear the sound of waves lapping the nearby shoreline. Minutes passed. He had nowhere to go. Time didn't matter. Checkers was soon purring and fast asleep. He looked down at the cat and smiled. *Here's to better days,* he thought. A short while later, Baxter had nodded off too. They'd both had a busy day.

Baxter rose early the next day after a hit of strong caffeine. He packed his guitar case and teaching materials into the back of his car and made his way to Clare High. Although the school was within walking distance, he decided to drive to ensure he wouldn't be late on his first day. The first thing he noticed upon entering the school grounds was the school motto printed on a sign: *per volar sunata* - an Italian phrase which translates as 'born to soar.' This immediately made him think of The Eagles, the American band who had recorded a string of amazing songs over the past few years. Baxter waltzed into the school office, clutching his acoustic guitar humming their song 'Already Gone', which, in turn, made his own mood soar!

'May I help you?' asked the stylish, forty-something-year-old lady from behind a small wooden desk.

'I'm Nathan Baxter, and I'm starting today,' he announced. She looked around her desk and lifted some papers, accidentally knocking over a small pot of glue. 'I'm the new music teacher,' he added with a smile, holding up the guitar case. She returned his smile.

'Of course you are. Lovely to meet you, Nathan, I'm Phillipa, but everyone calls me Pip,' she said, extending her arm.

'Well, I will too, Pip,' he replied, shaking her hand.

Baxter's commencement at Clare High could be summed up in one word: questions. He had lots of them, which was only to be expected on the first day. However there were no first-day nerves and he quickly felt like this new teaching gig was meant to be. Nat believed in his ability to teach music and was confident that he could make a positive impact at the new school. That's not to say it was all smooth sailing on day one at his new employer by the sea. A couple of kids in his Grade 8 class were rowdy and tested him, but that was to be expected and part of the territory when filling the shoes of a previous teacher. Interestingly enough, most of the students in his classes brought their recorders with them to school.

'It's a start,' mused Nat, as he listened to some horrendous interpretations of well-known nursery rhymes and even a Christmas carol!

'Great effort there, guys and gals, but if you played that in a snow-covered Swedish village on Christmas Eve, the locals would indeed be wishing for a 'silent night.' Although his comment drew a humorous reaction, Baxter could see boredom on many of their faces. They were uninterested and played with little emotion, no doubt having learned those songs only because they'd had to. During the Grade 10 lesson, Baxter waved his arms wildly in the air and stopped the class mid-song. He then took a seat at the front of the classroom with his guitar resting on his lap.

'Is anyone here actually enjoying what it is you are playing?' he asked. No hands were raised.

'OK, put your recorders down for a moment, and let's try this,' he said, then began strumming the chords of 'Hey Jude'.

'Put your shyness to one side, and please join in by singing the chorus; try to feel the emotion of the song.' Some of the teens looked at each other and chuckled, unsure of what to make of the situation. Then one by one, and eventually all of the class joined in, singing in unison on the Beatles' hit from 1968. Watching his new students sing loudly on one of Lennon and McCartney's masterpieces brought back memories of his Swedish friends Brigitta and Edvard, which then led to an image of Amber. He quickly shook the thought aside and refocused on his guitar playing. At the song's conclusion, most of the class were smiling and in a jovial mood. Thanks to John and Paul, he had won them over in only a few minutes.

'Well done, everyone!' hollered Nat. 'You won't be needing those recorders in class from now on. I'm asking the Principal to obtain some acoustic guitars and sheet music for you, so start thinking about your favourite songs which you'd like to learn to play.'
The kids all cheered, and as they exited the classroom, a couple of them even shook their new teacher's hand. Two girls approached Nat's desk and thanked him for introducing something interesting to the class. One of the girls, whose name was Sylvie, was wearing a Rod Stewart tee-shirt and spoke with a slight French accent.

'Mr. Bahkstere, I sink ze Beatles are great, but do you like someone like ze Rod Stewart? I suppose you sink he's somewhat of a poseur, no?' asked Sylvie, glancing at her classmate for support.

'Au contraire, mademoiselle. Rod rocks - he's a great frontman who sings with a lot of soul. I saw him and The Faces when they toured Sweden in early 1970. They were really great,' replied Nathan. Sylvie's eyes widened and both girls giggled, pleased with their new teacher's reply. After the girls had left the classroom, Baxter sat behind his new desk and smiled, thinking back to *his* teenage days and how he used to play records in his bedroom until late. He'd swill cola and pore over album covers, such as *Out Of Our Heads* by the Stones, *A Hard Day's Night* by the Beatles, or that self-titled debut from The Kinks. *Music - the elixir of life,* he thought, exhaling a contented sigh. He returned his guitar to its case, gathered his paperwork and shut the classroom door behind him.

'How was your first day, Mr. Baxter?' asked Pip as he entered the school office. Nat placed his guitar down and smiled.

'Really great, I think this gig's going to work out fine,' he replied. 'And if I can call you Pip, then you have to call me Nat.' Pip blushed a little and cleared her throat.

'Thanks, Nat. Agreed. I heard singing earlier and saw some happy faces as the kids left the music room. I mentioned it to Mr. Naylor.' Baxter hadn't as yet met the school principal in person, a local man in his 40s who had been at the helm for over a decade.

'Is he in at the moment?' asked Nat, nodding at the Principal's office.

'Yes, he's just returned from bus duty. Go right in,' replied Pip.

Carl Naylor had lived in Clare for most of his life, and running the high school meant everything to him. Tall and thin with wavy grey hair, he was popular with the students and had the respect of his staff too. He was also a passionate sports fan who happily coached the school's basketball and football teams. On weekends, Carl could sometimes be seen behind the counter of Naylor's Fish and Chips, a busy food outlet in town that had been in his family for three generations. Popular with both locals and tourists, Nat had recently walked past the shop and was keen to sample some of their menu. After they exchanged pleasantries, Baxter steered the conversation toward the school's music curriculum.

'Y'know Carl, although younger children often enjoy learning to play the recorder, I feel that most modern teenagers find it tedious, as I observed in today's classes.'

'Oh really?' replied Carl. 'Your predecessor, Mrs. Doyle introduced that instrument, and the students would play them at our yearly Christmas concert. I've never heard any protests or backlash before.'

'Well, I think the kids are probably being polite or cannot be bothered complaining,' replied Baxter. Principal Naylor removed his reading glasses and looked Nat up and down before speaking.

'I take it you have a suggestion to remedy this apparent recorder-boredom?'
Nathan smiled, then leaned over and removed his acoustic guitar from its hardshell case. He rested the instrument on his knees, still smiling.

'Indeed I do, Mr. Naylor - indeed I do,' replied Nat, before performing an impromptu version of the Beatles' song 'Blackbird'. Baxter sang and looked down at his fret hand, as the school principal shifted uncomfortably in his seat - unsure of how to react to the situation. After a few moments though, the magic of the music enveloped him, and he nodded his head in time with the melody. Upon hearing the music, Pip and another teacher entered the office to investigate. After Nathan had finished the song, the others in the room applauded his performance. He looked up at them and smiled.

'Wow!' said Pip. 'I didn't know we were in the presence of musical greatness.' Nathan laughed aloud and shook his head in response.

'You're too kind,' replied Nat. 'I am competent, nothing more and believe me, there are many, many competent musicians out there.'

'Well I think you sounded superb!' bellowed Carl, as Pip nodded her agreement.

'I have a few Joan Baez LPs at home. Do you know any of her songs?' queried Pip.

Nat grinned, tapped his foot, then plucked out the intro to 'The Night They Drove Old Dixie Down' before singing the first verse. His smile widened when his trio of listeners joined in on the chorus, lifting the mood in the Principal's office which was buoyant when the song was over.

'That's the first time in my life I've done any public singing!' shrieked Pip. 'And it's such a great song.'

'You're right, it's a wonderful tune,' said Nat. 'Joan Baez does a great take, but it's originally written and recorded by Robbie Robertson and The Band - y'know, the guys who backed up Dylan?' Carl politely nodded, oblivious to Baxter's rock 'n' roll history lesson, but impressed with the passion with which his new teacher delivered it.

'I'm guessing, Nathan, it's guitars that you'd like to introduce to the curriculum?'

'You guessed right, Mr. Naylor,' replied Nat with a hopeful expression. The principal, still on a high from the impromptu performance, smirked, then quickly gave the thumbs-up.

'Sure, why not!' he said, shaking Nat's hand. 'I feel like it could be a welcome change which the students will find beneficial. Please see Phillipa tomorrow to get the paperwork sorted.' Nat was elated and graciously thanked his new boss.

When he arrived home, he found Checkers on the porch, sound asleep on the sofa. Exhausted, Nat placed his guitar case down and sat alongside his pet, rousing her from her sleep. She looked up at him and meowed her annoyance.

'Sorry, Check,' he offered, then rested his head back. The cat stood up, stretched her front legs, and jumped down from the sofa. She proceeded to then press her body against her weary owner's legs, weaving in and out of them before affectionately rubbing her head on his leather shoes.

'I know, I know, it's *middagsdags*,' said Nat, peering at Checkers with one eye. 'That's Swedish for 'it's dinner time' by the way.' The moggie looked up and yawned. 'Come on then,' he said, getting to his feet. As Checkers devoured her dinner, Nat grabbed a cold beer and a packet of salted pea-nuts, lit some incense, and brought the Hi-Fi to life. He shuf-fled back out to the porch and reacquainted himself with the sofa. The light was fading and the smell of the ocean blended in harmony with the scent of jasmine. He sighed and sunk lower into the sofa. 'Well today was a happy day,' mused Nat, taking a double swig of ale. 'A few more of these would be great thanks Lord,' he added, looking skyward. He pushed the heavy window up a couple of inches to hear Clapton clearer. One solitary star sat high in the sky and flickered. Nat sighed.

'This may not be mainline Florida, but it will do me just fine.'

When students entered Nat's classes the next day, they were greeted with music emanating from the school's portable record player. But it wasn't just any old record on the turntable; it was, in fact, a copy of the 7" which their new music teacher had recorded as a teenager - 'Pristine Heart'. The fact that he'd actually cut a vinyl record had the desired effect and most of the students were suitably impressed. It was a teaching method he had previously used to keep the kids engaged, and over the next few days, students were allowed to bring in their favourite 45s. Giving the kids the opportunity to stand in front of their peers and talk about their vinyl choice proved popular - and it became a theme that Baxter would employ throughout the school year. The anticipation of learning about their fellow students' musical preferences created a positive atmosphere, and the arrival of acoustic guitars in the classroom a few days later pushed the excitement level even higher! After several weeks, it was apparent to Nat that many of his students possessed basic musical abilities, such as tuning the guitar or recognising when the music was off-key. Most of them had also mastered simple chord progressions and strumming patterns. However, one of his grade 9 students, a boy named Richard Montgomery, was head and shoulders above the rest with his guitar-playing proficiency. Before Baxter's class, he'd never touched a guitar in his life. But his natural flair and the ease with which he accomplished Nat's in-class demonstrations had his teacher looking at him more closely. While the rest of his classmates were learning the chords to songs such as America's 'A Horse With No

Name,' Richard had figured out the guitar solo! He'd also quickly mastered songs like 'Angie' and 'Wild Horses' by the Stones, as well. Nat had sent a note home to Richard's parents, explaining the rapid progress their son had made, and invited them to meet with him, but there'd been no reply.

One Friday afternoon, Carl poked his head into the music room as Nat was finishing up.

'Hey boss,' said Baxter, looking up.

'Now I've told you not to call me that,' retorted Carl, pointing at Nat with a half-grin. Baxter bowed his head Japanese-style in a mock apology.

'Gomen nasai, Carl-san. How can I help?'

'I am glad you asked, Mr. Baxter, because it is your help that I require. Tomorrow afternoon, the Stingrays have a game over at Beldon, and I sure could use a spare pair of hands. I need someone to help me score and also with the warm-up.'

'Is that football?' queried the non-sports-loving Nat. Carl closed his eyes and sighed.

'Basketball, Mr. Baxter, basketball. The Stingrays are Clare High's basketball team, and tomorrow, we are playing the Beldon Barracudas in a big quarter-final game.'

Although Baxter had no idea where point guard stood or where the three-point line was located, he had not forgotten the trust which Carl had shown in him when he first started by purchasing those guitars. He also wanted to build a strong rapport with his boss, so with that in mind, agreed to help. Although committed, there was still a little wince in his reply as he found most sports really boring. In fact, the closest thing Baxter had done that resembled a team sport, was hitting the two-player button on a pinnie. However, once he'd agreed to help, the thought of doing something completely different grew on him, and he was now quite looking forward to it!

On Sunday he was excited to be spending time with Hanna, whom he hadn't seen for a fortnight. Nat currently had access to see his daughter every second Sunday and he missed her terribly. That feeling of loss was indescribable, but it was the everyday things he missed the most about not being a part of his little girl's world: not seeing her smiling face each day, not hearing her laughter or her footsteps first thing in the morning. Those things just ripped him apart. It was really tough on him, but he knew he had to find the inner strength to move forward. He had no answers, except to bury his head in music, focus on his teaching, and to try and remain strong. And now, of course, he had basketball in his life!

'Just wait until I tell Hanna that I was the scorekeeper at a basketball game!' he laughed.

| 5 |

Strawberry-swirl

Also located on the coast, but with a much larger population, Beldon was about a forty-five minute drive from Clare. Unbeknownst to Baxter, the two high schools shared a strong rivalry dating back several years and whether it was sports or overall academic achievements, competition between the two schools was fierce. Around 11:00AM on a sunny Saturday, Carl's sapphire-blue Triumph TR6 pulled into Nat's driveway. He honked his horn a couple of times, and Baxter hurried out, slamming the front door behind him.

'Nice wheels, boss,' he said, settling into the vehicle. Carl smiled and greeted Nat, silently accepting that he'd have to get used to being called 'boss' by his new music teacher.

'Yes, it is. I'd very much like a TR7, but for the moment, this model suits me just fine.'

'You ever heard of a Saab Sonett?' asked Nat. 'It was a sports car which the Swedes produced. My ex-wife used to own a cute little yellow number.'

Carl shook his head as he changed gears.

'No I haven't,' he answered.

Nat cracked open a can of cola he'd brought with him and took a swig. The sun was bright and he slid on his dark sunglasses. The mood was jovial between the new colleagues as they cranked the volume on the cassette player and traversed the coastal highway. Baxter tapped his fingers on his knee in time with the music. He reached for the cassette case behind the driver's seat, unsnapped the lock and took a closer look at the titles.

'Johnny Cash, Chuck Berry, Gene Vincent, Elvis….you've got some great tapes in here, boss,' said Nat, nodding his approval.

'Well thank you, Mr. Baxter. That means a lot coming from you. I know you have immense knowledge of rock 'n' roll, and the students really value your opinion.' The music teacher grinned, pleased with the compliment and returned the cassette case to the rear of the vehicle. Although it was late autumn, the weather was glorious, and the sandy beaches they passed had attracted large gatherings of beachgoers. Carl raised the volume on the Gene Vincent track 'Be-Bop-A-Lula' and, to Nathan's surprise, started singing loudly on the chorus!

'Y'know Gene Vincent was a big influence on the Beatles, especially their early days. Lennon also covered 'Be-Bop-A-Lula' on his 1975 album *Rock 'n' Roll*,' said Nat. They swung onto the main street of Beldon, and the blue Triumph came to a halt at a traffic light.

'Nathan, how do you know so much about music?'

Carl asked. Silence. Ten seconds passed. 'You OK son?'

For Nathan Baxter, time stood still as he felt his heart melt. His gaze was fixed on a pretty young woman with long dark hair standing near the taxi rank. She was wearing a blue and white summer dress, with a black leather handbag draped over her shoulder. On her wrist was a floral print hair scrunchie. He noted the elegant way she stood with one hand clasped around the other. With her poise and beauty, she stood out from the crowd of people rushing past and Nat was mesmerised. Just as the traffic light changed to green, she caught Nathan's gaze, and for a brief moment, they locked eyes. Baxter looked back at her as the car surged forward.

'Everything OK, Nathan?' Carl asked again.

'Uh yeah, wow! She was beautiful,' replied Nat. 'Did you see her?'

'Who was?' quizzed Carl. 'I had my eyes on the road.'

'That girl back there, waiting for a taxi - she had *something* about her. I can't explain it,' said Nat. Carl turned the music down. 'I guess the last thing I need right now is a new lady in my life. Besides, I already have two, and there's no room for another one!' he laughed. His conservative older colleague looked at him, unsure of what to say in response. Nat looked back at him over his sunglasses. 'My daughter Hanna, and Checkers, my cat - those two girls take up all of my life,' he explained. Carl burst into laughter as they arrived at the basketball centre. For Baxter though, the incident with the lady at the taxi rank stayed with him, and was a reminder that, although he was nearly thirty, he still had a lot of love to give if he could find that special someone.

Nat enjoyed the basketball game more than he thought he would and was surprised by the level of passion Carl showed from the sidelines. At times, his boss was quite animated, waving his hands in the air while shouting instructions to his players. The Barracudas beat the Stingrays 73-58, and Carl made sure all players congratulated the victors. He chatted all the way back to Clare, still on a high from the game.

'Thanks for helping out today, Nathan,' he said, pulling up at the kerb outside Baxter's house. 'It's just a shame we couldn't beat them.'

'We'll get 'em next time, boss...err coach,' he said with a wink. 'See you on Monday.' As the TR6 drove away, Baxter heard the bell on Checkers' collar jingling louder as she jumped from the sofa and hurried towards him. Her hunger-filled meows gained strength as she followed her owner through the front door. After fixing dinner for the two of them, Nat burned some incense, cracked open a beer, gathered his AM radio, then soaked in the bath for an hour.

The sound of light rain tapping on the roof woke him early the next morning. However, grey skies and the forecast of more rain were not going to dampen his day's plans. Because today was the second Sunday of the month, which meant spending a few hours with his little angel, Hanna. He'd recently finalised child custody arrangements with his ex-wife, which meant he now had regular fortnightly access, as well as half of Hanna's school holidays. That suited Nat fine, as when the school kids were on break, so were the teachers!

Pulling up to his former marital house after the split always felt...strange. Feelings of frustration and anger had subsided some time ago, giving way to fatigue and sadness. He also lamented the fact that, after all they'd been through - and they *had* been through a lot, and shared many happy memories - they couldn't have parted as friends. Amber had made it clear, though, that an ongoing, amicable friendship was not going to happen. The fact that he had not entered the property, instead remaining in his vehicle on the street, was a stark reminder of that. *It could be so different,* he thought.

The sound of voices made him look up and he saw Hanna exit the house. She walked along the driveway towards him with her head down. Her long hair was tied back and she was carrying a *Snoopy* suitcase and matching drink bottle.

'Daddy!' she shrieked, running into his outstretched arms. He picked her up, greeting her with a tight hug. She giggled loudly and he kissed her on the cheek.

'It's *soooo* nice to see you, honey,' he said, holding her high in the air. She squealed and clung onto her Dad's neck. 'Come on, let's get moving. The fun starts now.' Hanna clapped with delight, as he secured her in the front seat, then shut the car door. Nathan glanced towards the house and saw the living room curtain quickly close. He shook his head and sighed. As the weather was miserable, he took Hanna to the bowling alley for a couple of hours, followed by lunch at Frida's Fried Chicken, where, according to Hanna (and her friends) they sold the *best* chicken burgers in the world! After devouring one himself, Nathan was in agreement, but also rated their chocolate thick shakes highly as well! He sat back in the booth and tapped his stomach in contentment. After shopping for some new books, they rounded off the day with a visit to the ice cream parlour.

'Strawberry-swirl is the best,' exclaimed Hanna, with ice cream smeared around her mouth and chin.

'No way,' retorted Nathan, wiping her face with a napkin. 'My all-time favourite is jaffa, however chocolate is what's known as a fail-safe flavour. You know what you're gonna get, and it wins every time.' Hanna smiled up at him and he touched her on the nose. He had really missed her and was starting to feel blue. 'Hey, I must buy Checkers some cat food before we go back to Mum's,' he said, pushing away any impending thoughts of sadness. 'She's such a lazy puss, all she does is eat and sleep.' Hanna watched her Dad closely as he spoke. 'Checkers isn't much of a watchdog, ahm, I mean a watchcat,' he said with a shrug and a smirk. His attempted joke brought on a fit of giggles from her which filled him with warmth. He put his head to one side and smiled. *What an angel,* he thought. *I am truly blessed.*

Half an hour later, he returned Hanna to her home. Nathan watched as she walked away and waved back at him. He hated saying goodbye to his daughter. It was a feeling he loathed and one he would never get used to - ever. It was like switching a light off in his heart - a feeling that life was momentarily drawn out of him. He knocked a Clapton cassette into the tape deck and made his way back to Clare.

The rain continued throughout the evening, but by early morning it had dissipated, and the storm cell had moved out to sea. Baxter stopped in at Nugget's for coffee and donuts before making his way to school. He was still on a high after spending time with Hanna and he strode into the staff room in a positive frame of mind. After making another coffee, he made his way to the music room and was surprised to hear the sweet sound of a guitar flowing out from it. He stopped outside the classroom and listened, searching his brain for the song. It was familiar, and he knew those chords backwards, but just couldn't place it. He shut his eyes and listened some more. Of course! It was Neil Young's 'Old Man'. Baxter walked in, singing the chorus, as Richard looked up and stopped playing, dropping his plectrum in the process. There were three other students looking on.

'No no, don't stop brother, that's sounding great!' said Nathan. Richard smiled, continued strumming, and man oh man, he *did* sound great - note-perfect in fact. Baxter looked on in admiration while continuing to chime in on the chorus. When the lesson was over, Nat called Richard over to his desk before the students exited the classroom.

'Hey Richard, I'm just chasing up that note which I sent home for your parents, as I haven't heard anything back from them.' Richard lowered his head, mumbled something and stood uncomfortably, shifting from side to side. Surveying his body language, Baxter could sense there might be an underlying problem. 'Y'know, I've been immersed in the world of music all my life, especially guitars, and you, my friend, have an abundance of natural talent.' Richard half-smiled, embarrassed by the compliment and wasn't sure where to look. 'What are your plans after leaving school? Have you considered a career in music?' Nat asked. The teenager paused for a moment before answering.

'No I haven't, Mr. Baxter,' he hushed, scratching his

head before pausing again. Nathan gave him a few moments to reply. 'But I really love playing the guitar; it makes me happy. I practice until my fingers bleed, and it's the one thing in life that makes me feel alive. Do you know what I mean?' They looked at each other. His teacher nodded and smiled.

'I do, absolutely I do. The guitar is my life too, and music has always been there for me, so yes, I very much understand.'

'Well, my folks, ahm, they don't understand,' replied Richard. 'Especially my Dad. He thinks music is a waste of time and wants me to work in the family business. I gave him your note, but he ripped it up.'

'Is that so?' replied Baxter in dismay. He tapped a pencil on his desk for several seconds, deep in thought. He then walked to the blackboard, picked up a piece of chalk and scrawled four words: *National Academy of Music*

Nat underlined the words to emphasise his point before speaking.

'Brother, with lots of practice and determination, *this* could be your next step after completing high school. Where your musical journey goes from there is up to you.'

Richard nodded while contemplating this. 'I will talk this over with Mr. Naylor. Maybe a telephone call from him could help sway your parents.' The student smiled and picked up his guitar case.

'Thanks, Mr. Baxter. I'd appreciate that.'

Nat only had two classes that day, so spent the remainder of the Monday in the staff room grading homework. He didn't feel like cooking or sampling more of the greasy treats at Nugget's, so after work, ventured into The Southern Anchor, the oldest pub in Clare. He found a window seat and ordered steak with mushroom sauce, and boy, did it taste great! After finishing off his beer, he contemplated something sweet from the dessert menu but decided to pass. Nat ordered a cup of coffee instead and sat looking at the harbour lights. He heard the pleasant-sounding, recognisable harmonies of ABBA playing on a nearby radio and shut his eyes. It made him think of Stockholm, the Swedish capital where ABBA called home. His mind drifted back to the start of the decade when he and Amber had visited there. They'd caught a train early one Saturday morning and spent several hours travelling across the country. But any fond memories of that first day in the capital were tarnished by an incident which happened not long after their arrival. After checking into their hotel, they had strolled through a busy local market-place. While waiting for Amber outside a public toilet, Nat was distracted by the sight of some used records at a nearby stall. Consequently, when Amber exited the bathroom, she could not find him and they became separated. After half an hour they eventually met up, but she was fuming. His apologies fell on deaf ears and she refused to talk to him for much of that afternoon. Looking back, these were warning signs of Amber's personality which Baxter didn't pay enough attention to. She was dominant, and he was soft and easygoing, so he would usually end up accepting blame and apologising. These incidents increased over the years, forming small cracks that would ultimately lead to a crumbling marriage. The sound of the waitress placing the coffee cup on his table jolted him, and he sat bolt upright.

'Oh, I'm sorry, Sir. I didn't mean to startle you,' she said. Nat smiled and rubbed his hand over his forehead.

'No, no, it's OK. I was miles away, lost in the past.'

'Well, I hope you find your way back,' she added.

'Oh I did, I did, and I've never seen things more clearly,' he replied.

He stirred sugar into his hot coffee and looked back at the lights. The wind had picked up, and the small fishing boats were bobbing up and down like wine corks in water. As he exited the pub, he bumped into Pip, who was dining with her sister. After making small talk for five minutes, Baxter bid farewell and headed home. He was beat.

Over the next month, Nat immersed himself in his work, determined to remain positive and ensure that his coastal relocation was a success. That's not to say it was all smooth sailing as some classes were rough - mostly caused by unruly students. Teenage attitude? Sure. Issues at home? Possibly. No interest in being at school? Maybe. Neverthe-less, Baxter made sure that every one of those kids in his classes had the chance to get their hands on a guitar and the opportunity to feel the sensation of creating music through sound - even if that meant running through repetitive chord progressions. Nathan brought his acoustic guitar to school each day, but to liven things up, would often haul in his JTM45 Marshall amp, plug in his '59 Les Paul and let fly! The kids roared their approval as he blasted through tunes like The Who's 'Behind Blue Eyes', much to the annoyance of Miss McDonnell and her mathematics class next door! She would often march into the Principal's office and complain about the noise. Carl, standing near Pip's desk, frowned and shook his head disapprovingly at Nat as he exited for the day, lugging his guitars and amp along with him.

'Sorry, boss,' said Baxter, winking at Pip. 'I'll keep the volume down next time.' The music teacher was in good spirits as he loaded the gear into his car. Besides it being Friday, he had that tune by The Who stuck in his brain and sang it loudly while driving home. He was also going to see Hanna again on Sunday and was really looking forward to spending more time with her. Seeing as how it was Friday (and he had no other plans), he thought he'd check out the town's other pub - The Seahorse Inn.

Cheap and cheerful, the tavern was popular with locals and was one of the only late-night openers in town. Baxter had skipped lunch, so by the time he descended the flight of stairs which led to the tavern, he was starving. He was also keen for an end-of-week drink. As Nathan entered, he noted the thick, dark-blue carpet on the floor and pondered if it was meant to resemble the sea. He also spied a jukebox, dartboard, pool table and pinball machines as he approached the bar. He leaned over to see what beer they had on tap just as the barmaid emerged from the kitchen. She was carrying a large tray on which sat some clean beer glasses, a bowl of green beans, and a bag of peanuts.

'What will it be?' she asked with a sunshine smile. Her name was Charli, a local girl born and raised in Clare. She was petite, with curly red hair that went down to her waist. Baxter looked up and smiled back at her.

'Do you have Ashton Ale on tap?'

'Sure do,' replied Charli. 'Glass, chū-jockey, or dai-jockey?' she asked, holding up a couple of different-sized beer jugs.

'Erm, I'll get the big one,' answered Baxter, unsure of what the barmaid had asked. Charli giggled as she began to fill the large glass jug.

'The owner of the pub is Noriko, a Japanese lady who has run the place since the mid- '70s. It was previously called The Taco Tavern and was a Japanese-themed bar,' she explained. 'However the business went belly-up, but we still use lots of the old stuff - like beer glasses.' Charli placed a coaster in front of Nat and set the dai-jockey down. Baxter handed over some cash, raised the large glass, and immersed his lips in the frothy head. As he tilted his neck back, he noticed a framed cartoon of a grinning green seahorse, holding a beer, perched high above the bar. Adjacent to the drawing was a signed 8 x 10 of a Japanese singer named Kiyoshi Maekawa. What caught Baxter's attention, though, was the signed record hanging above it. He strained to make out the title: *Jailhouse Rock* by Akiko Wada. He took a second mouthful and rested the glass down. Charli placed the bowl of green beans in front of him, and he looked at them curiously.

'It's called edamame,' she explained, picking one up and popping the soybean contained within, into her mouth. 'In Japan, these are a popular snack when drinking beer. That's what Noriko told me.' Nat plucked one of the long beans up and copied her, enjoying the sweet, nutty flavour. He then refocused his attention on the beer.

'It kinda reminds me of a beer stein which they have in parts of Europe,' he said, tapping the glass with his finger.

'I guess,' said Charli, shrugging her shoulders. 'But I've never left the country, so I'll take your word for it, Mr...'

'Baxter, Nathan Baxter,' he replied, after another large gulp. 'I'm the new music te...'

'Teacher at Clare High,' finished Charli. He looked at her, open-mouthed. 'It's a small town; news travels fast, and everyone knows everyone else's business,' she added, giggling again. At that moment, the kitchen doors swung open, and a short Japanese lady rushed by, carrying a tray of piping hot chicken wings.

'Charli, *isoide! Isoide!* she said urgently. The barmaid laughed and looked back at Nathan.

'*Isoide* means *hurry* in Japanese,' she explained.

'That's right,' interrupted Noriko. 'It sure does, and happy hour is about to begin, so you need to get back to work and not spend all your time talking to customers. Even handsome ones,' she finished, giving Nathan a cheeky wink. He smiled politely at her and then took another gulp from his giant beer glass.

'Hi, I'm Nathan, new resident of Clare,' he said, extending his arm.

'The new high school music teacher? Pleased to meet you; I'm Noriko,' she replied, shaking his outstretched hand. 'I've been in Clare for some time now. I'm originally from Sasebo in Japan, which, like Clare, is also on the water, only the population is bigger. It's home to over two hundred thousand people. Slightly busier than here!' she said, laughing.

'How did you end up in a small coastal town like Clare, then?' asked Nat, taking another large swig. Noriko paused and tilted her head to one side, searching for a memory.

'I used to operate a snack bar in Sasebo. One day, a handsome sailor walks in - one thing led to another, and a year or so later, I am married and living in Clare! Only problem was, the sailor-boy was at sea a lot and had a girl in every port! Sayonara, buddy. So, he left, and I stayed.'

'Wow, that's quite a story. Your barmaid Charli over there just told me you also owned a Japanese bar?'

'Uh huh, I did,' nodded Noriko. She then motioned for Charli to go and serve Pam and Denise, two regulars who had sat down at a nearby table. 'Anyway, after he'd split, I needed an income and didn't want to go back to Japan. So, I found this place, which was a *real* dump, and turned it into a cool sea-side pub with the feel of home.' Nat scooped up a handful of peanuts and watched Noriko as she slowly poured herself a glass of lemonade.

'...and then?' he asked impatiently.

'The Japanese word for octopus is *taco*, which I thought would be a brilliant name for my new establishment - especially as we're right on the ocean. So I called the place The Taco Tavern. The only problem was, most people thought it was a Mexican restaurant! As a result, the business bombed and most nights we'd shut early. We nearly went bankrupt. But after a couple of years, we had a name change, things picked up, and we're still in business.' Noriko raised her glass and clinked it loudly with Nat's dai-jockey. '*Kampai!* she said with a broad grin.

'Cheers!' replied Baxter. He finished his beer, ordered another from Noriko and asked for some change. Armed with a pocketful of coins, he stepped down from the barstool and made his way to the pinball machines. Prior to playing the silver ball, he rolled some coins into the jukebox. He teed up George Harrison's 'Ding Dong,' Cheap Trick's 'Surrender,' followed by Clapton with 'Cocaine,' and The Babys with 'Isn't It Time.' After downing four dai-jockeys of beer and a large complimentary glass of shōchū from Noriko, Baxter was starting to feel quite drunk. He rolled one final coin into the jukebox and stood over it as George Harrison's slide guitar welcomed the song 'Give Me Love (Give Me Peace on Earth).' Nathan took an uneasy swig from his glass and gulped down the ale. He stared blankly at the machine's flashing lights, somewhat frozen by Harrison's lyrics.

'Everything OK, Nathan? Do you need another drink?' asked Charli, sauntering past. Nat looked over at her and smiled. She politely returned the smile.

Man, that smile of hers is infectious he thought. 'A smile that could melt a snowman's heart,' he whispered. 'No, I'm good, thanks Charli. Besides, I'd better get outta here; it's getting kinda late,' he slurred.

'Well, you come back soon, OK?' said the pretty young redhead.

Baxter exited The Seahorse Inn and staggered out onto the quiet street. Although he was full of alcohol, his stomach moaned loudly for food. Of course, he could have ordered some of those tasty chicken wings he'd seen Noriko carrying earlier, but found himself trapped in that magical world of flippers, bumpers, targets, and ramps. Nugget's was shut, as was Naylor's Fish and Chips, which was probably for the best, as being served by the boss while intoxicated was not a great career move. There was a solitary petrol station at the end of town that often stayed open, but only if Mick the mechanic worked late - and the menu there consisted of chewing gum, lifesavers, potato chips, and a solitary drink machine. That was about it. The only option available was the Paradise Pizza Parlour, which was a couple of blocks away. There was always the fall-back option of grilled cheese on toast back home, but Nat shrugged off that idea. He laughed at nothing in particular, hooked his thumbs in the belt loops of his jeans and headed for the pizza joint. He arrived just in time, as the place was empty and about to close up. Gino, the owner, was grateful for the late-night order as it had been a quiet evening. Baxter ordered a large bacon, ham, and mushroom pizza with garlic bread and began eating while walking home. Light rain began to fall, so he quickened his pace while attempting to pull his jacket up over his head, all the while clutching the pizza and bread. Losing his balance, Nathan fell drunkenly to the ground, causing half of the pizza to spill out of the box. The garlic bread landed a couple of metres away. Baxter sat up and laughed, then cleaned up the spilled pizza before reboxing it.

'Still looks OK to me,' he muttered, before snatching up the garlic bread and continuing his journey home. Drunk and damp, he navigated the front porch steps, rested the food on the sofa, and located his house keys. Nat heard the famil-iar, welcoming sound of Checkers' bell and looked up as she darted out from the side of the house. 'Sorry buddy,' he said. 'Here, you must be starving.' he added, and rested a large slice of pizza on the ground. Checkers immediately got to work on the late dinner as her owner let himself in the house. He stopped at the fridge and hauled out a bottle of cola from the side shelf. Exhausted, Baxter kicked off his shoes and sat up in bed, devouring the rest of the pizza and garlic bread. It was one of the best pizzas he'd eaten. Still hungry and wishing he had ordered the family size, Nat picked away at the remnants of melted cheese stuck to the inside of the box. He washed down the meal with large, contented gulps of cola, belched, wiped his mouth, then dropped the empty box onto the floor. The room began to spin as he sunk his head down in the pillow. He let out a groan and lightly touched his pounding temple. For a brief moment, feelings of sadness entered his mind, but he channelled Beatle George and chanted a positive mantra to keep them at bay. Although it didn't help his vertigo much, it had the desired effect. He pictured little Hanna and smiled.

| 6 |

Alana

Nathan woke the next day feeling seedy, with a bad case of desert-mouth. After guzzling what felt like a litre of water, he collapsed back into bed. He placed one of his dirty socks across his eyes to remedy the bright sunlight streaming in from below the curtains, and fell back to sleep. Finally surfacing at a quarter to four, he changed into some board shorts, grabbed a towel from the bathroom and headed for the beach. He passed Checkers on the porch, curled up in a ball, sound asleep on the sofa. He studied her, out to the world, with her front paws gently curled. He smiled. *My little ray of sunshine - basking in the sunshine.* The beach was only a few minutes' walk and apart from a lone fisherman, was deserted. Baxter waded out and dove under an incoming wave. The rush of cold, salty water on his face was refreshing, giving his mind and body a much-needed recharge. After half an hour or so in the surf, the winter sun began to set, and the weather turned cool, bringing with it a soothing light rain. He wrapped the towel around his waist and made his way home. Hanna once asked him why his bath towels were like 'toast', a result of her bachelor-Dad being blissfully unaware of fabric softener. Consequently, the term 'toast towels' was born, a thought which brought a smile to his face.

Once home, he soaked in a hot bath, with an ale and the transistor radio for company. As the door was ajar, Checkers wandered in, meowed, then rubbed her head on the bottom rail.

'I know, I know,' said Nat. 'You're hungry. Give me a moment, buddy,' he added, wrenching himself from the tub. She exited the room and headed for the kitchen. Nat walked in shortly thereafter, dropping water on the floor as he moved about.

'Aha!' he yelped, spying a can of tinned food at the back of the cupboard. 'This must've been left by the previous tenant,' he uttered, opening the sausage-vegetable mixture. He poured half into Checkers' bowl, watching it ooze from the can. The cat made short work of the dinner before requesting an outside visit. Baxter heated up the remainder of the slop on the stove and spread it over some toast. He poured ketchup over the meal, so that if it *was* past its use-by-date, it would primarily be the taste of tomato he'd cop.

Still hungry after his meal, Baxter walked to the milk bar and returned with some salt and vinegar chips along with salted peanuts. He gently placed Melanie's *Photograph* album on the Hi-Fi and settled into the sofa on the porch. Nat owned all of Melanie's albums, but that particular record was one he always returned to. He rested his head back, shut his eyes, and breathed in the salt air. He could hear the soothing sound of waves lapping on the shoreline, bringing with it a feeling of calm. Tomorrow, he was seeing Hanna and he was excited. Maybe they'd get some candy, or he'd take her for a milkshake? He placed his acoustic guitar on his lap and strummed aimlessly. He yawned and looked skyward. The rain had passed, but the cloud cover prevented any star-gazing. The evening air was getting cold, so at 11:30PM, Nathan blew out the candle and headed inside to get some shut-eye.

Baxter's sleep was interrupted by Checkers tapping at his bedroom window in the early hours. He then found it difficult to get back to sleep, and lay there for quite some time with his arms behind his head, listening to the nearby ocean. He could also hear semi-trailers in the distance, dropping gears as they descended a mountain road some miles away. Nat eventually fell back to sleep before the alarm roused him from his rest. He poured Checkers some warm milk, brewed fresh coffee and strode to his car. Checkers followed him, meowing her resistance while darting around his feet.

'Sorry, Check. I'm off to meet Hanna. I'll be back later this afternoon. Hopefully, you can see her during the school holidays.' His cat returned to the porch and watched as her owner reversed out of the driveway. Baxter knocked a cassette into the car stereo, raised the volume, and roared off. It was one of many purchases he'd scored the previous pay day from the local music store, Clare's Records and Tapes, which was owned by a local music buff coincidentally named Clare! He held the cassette case at arm's length and grinned. *Aerosmith, live - does it get any better?'* he asked, as Joe Perry's driving guitar riff signalled the arrival of the song 'Chip Away the Stone'. 'Hell yeah!' exclaimed Nat, singing along with vocalist Steven Tyler whilst banging on the steering wheel.

As he neared Port Stafford, his stomach growled for food, so he stopped in at a milk bar for a toasted sandwich. Upon exiting the shop, he passed a telephone booth and called Amber to confirm his arrival time.

'Didn't you get my message?' she said.

'No, what message?' he replied. 'I didn't receive any message.'

'I phoned your school late yesterday. Hanna is attending a classmate's birthday party today,' she said coolly.

'But that's not fair, Amber, and that's not what we agreed on,' replied Nat, frustration evident in his voice. 'And I'm already on my way!'

'I gave you the message. Why can't you get a telephone like most normal people?' she hissed. He closed his eyes and pursed his lips. She swore at him in Swedish and he heard the handset being passed.

'Hi Daddy,' said Hanna in a bright voice. 'Sorry, I can't see you today.'

'Hi honey,' he said, 'I was looking forward to seeing you, and I miss you.'

'Tell him you will see him during the school holidays,' he heard his ex-wife say. Hanna duly repeated the words that her mother had uttered. His head dropped and that familiar feeling of despair washed over him. Silence.

'Daddy? Are you there? I'm going to a birthday party, and I'm wearing a new dress!' said Hanna excitedly.

'It's OK, angel. That sounds like a lot of fun, and yes,

I'll see you soon during the school holidays. Come to Clare and have a sleepover at Dad's house; Checkers will be really happy to see you,' he replied. Hanna giggled.

'Bye Daddy.'

'Bye, Hanna. Daddy loves you,' he added, before the call cut out. He sighed and tapped his knuckle for a moment on the glass window of the phone box. He composed himself and walked back inside the store to buy a drink. For the next half hour, Nathan sat in his car, chugging from a cola bottle while listening to classical music. It helped him relax. The sun was shining, so he put on his dark glasses and stepped out of the car for a moment to stretch. He watched as a young family of four walked past him. They had twin daughters, who were about the same age as Hanna. The father nodded at Nathan and he returned it. As if in slow motion, he watched them enter the store when suddenly, a wave of realisation slapped him sideways - it was a visual reminder of something he would never have. Feelings of guilt, anger, remorse, failure, sadness and relief all hammered his mind from different angles. He shook his head to clear the thoughts. 'I've done nothing wrong,' he said aloud. 'And I just wanted to be happy. We were both unhappy.' Nat exhaled, outstretched his arms, and strode to the garbage bin with the empty bottle. He tossed it in and stared into space, oblivious to the fact that the family were now watching him. He half-smiled, held his head up, and returned to his vehicle.

He drove in silence for most of the way back to Clare.

One thought that frequently occupied his mind was the compatibility of couples based on shared interests. This was usually followed by a string of 'what ifs' related to his own life; What if, early in his relationship with Amber, he hadn't ignored the times when he'd felt uncomfortable? What if they had've talked through issues as they arose? What if he had've pursued Amber's friend, Karita? She was into rock 'n' roll at least. He sighed.

'You are the master of your own ship,' he reaffirmed. *'I think that's how it goes. Is that what Kimberly told me?'* he thought, recalling the conversation he'd had back at South Fletcher High with his former colleague. 'If that's the case, then, are we currently off course?' he asked, clicking the radio on. 'And I don't mind being off course, or even on a new course, so long as the damn waters are smooth.' The faster vehicles overtook him as he coasted for home - and it *was* beginning to feel like home - and that made him feel a little better.

'Home,' Baxter murmured without emotion. 'Home,' he repeated, this time in a trance-like state. He found the yellow lines on the road captivating as his thoughts began to backtrack. He recalled the times late in his marriage when he'd purposely work after school - grading papers, preparing lessons, hell, even cleaning the blackboards for other teachers. Eventually, he'd board a late-night bus; but the uneasy feeling that nagged at him was growing, and would soon be something he could no longer ignore. 'I'm going home to a house, but not a home,' Nat said aloud, recalling his back-of-the-bus mindset. He once again shook his head as if to clear the memories, then cranked the volume as The Who ripped out of the rear speakers with 'Won't Get Fooled Again'. 'I hear ya Daltrey, I hear ya,' said Nat, echoing the vocalist's lyrics.

Baxter stopped in at the grocery store, grabbed two lock-necks of Ashton Ale, a steak and mushroom pie, chocolate bar, and a can of sardines for Checkers. Once home, he slept for a couple of hours and then grabbed the chilled beers, a book of poetry, a notebook, and pencil before making his way to the beach. Before exiting, he gathered a matchbook off the porch table, shoving it in his rear pocket. Once again, he had the beach all to himself, apart from a couple of fishermen who were some distance away. There was about an hour and a half of sunlight left, the air was cool, and the sky hazy. He sat on a large log, tightened his denim jacket for warmth and gathered some pieces of driftwood for a fire. After a couple of failed attempts, the fire gained strength and Nat sat closer to the dancing flames.

'Hanna would love doing this,' he sighed. 'Maybe we'll light a fire during the school holidays.' He wrenched open a beer and took a swig. He read a few pages from the book, but his attention was drawn to some seagulls, shrieking as they balanced in the wind. Baxter studied them closely. Removing his pencil, he jotted down the phrase *Crying Seabirds*, and worked on some lines of his own. Nat's thoughts were interrupted by the unannounced yet friendly arrival of a small brown dog, who sniffed around his shoes.

'It's OK, she won't bite you,' said a voice to his right. He looked up and his heart skipped a beat. It was the pretty girl he had seen near the taxi rank in Beldon a few weeks back! Nat sat there petting the small dog with his heart thumping out of his chest. He needed to say something but was struck by nerves. Taking another swig of beer, he wiped his mouth and cleared his throat.

'I have a cat named Checkers,' he uttered, then silently groaned at his awkward comment. She smiled warmly in his direction.

'That's a very cute name. Her name is Button,' replied the girl, nodding at her dog. 'She's a maltese terrier, six months old.'

Baxter couldn't take his eyes off this woman.

'I'm Nathan,' he said, extending his hand.

'Hi Nathan, my name's Alana,' she replied. The wind had grown stronger, whipping her hair across her face. She removed a scrunchie from her wrist and tied back her long, dark locks. Nat watched her face reflecting the glow of the fire. She was beautiful.

'Do you live around here?' asked Alana.

'Yes, I moved to Clare quite recently and I love it. It's really nice here.'

'I'm from Beldon - born and raised,' she replied. 'I've been coming over to Clare a lot recently, to walk Button and to also think and clear my mind.'

'Well, the isolation of the beach and sound of the waves is an ideal place for that. I find solace here,' replied Nat. She nodded slowly, sensing there was something special about him. 'Will you join me?' he asked, inviting her to sit down. Her eyes were now fixed on his, and she broke into a shy smile. Alana sat down next to Nathan on the log as Button lay in front of the fire. 'I'd offer you a beer, only I don't have a glass,' he said, holding up the second bottle.

'It's fine. I learnt poise and elegance when I was a

ballerina, so even without a beer glass, I *think* I can manage to drink gracefully from a bottle,' she said with a smirk.

'A ballerina! Wow, how lovely,' he exclaimed, handing her the bottle after opening it. 'I've read that a dancer's life is dedicated to training and total commitment.'

'It's true. You have to make many sacrifices. I began dancing when I was 4 years old and have devoted my life to ballet. I retired from professional dancing a year ago after a series of injuries. Over the years, I've recovered from quite a few fractures in my feet, but a back injury restricted my ability to dance fluently and although I've recovered, it ended my career.' she explained, putting her head down. Sensing her sadness, he put more driftwood on the fire and then raised his bottle for a toast.

'I think you should be proud of all you have achieved Alana. I bet you were among the best ballet dancers in the country, right? That is outta sight and really impressive! You made it!' he said, clinking her bottle. She lifted her head up and nodded.

'I guess...' she said softly, pondering his comment. 'What about you, Nathan? How do you spend your days?'

'Well, I too have made a career from moving about in front of an audience, but not as stylish and graceful as you, I imagine. I'm a guitar player - a music teacher, and I currently teach at Clare High,' he replied. 'Music is my life. Ever since I was a kid.'

Alana smiled at him.

'You look just like a guitar player,' she replied, taking a sip of beer. 'I know very little about rock 'n' roll and wish

I knew more about music. Of course, I'm familiar with ballet scores like *The Rite of Spring, The Nutcracker,* and *Swan Lake'.*

Baxter scratched his head.

'I know of Greg Lake from King Crimson and ELP....and Swan Song, that's Led Zeppelin and Bad Company's label.' She shrugged and laughed. He laughed too. They talked until it was dark. Nathan could feel an energy with Alana as he walked her to her car. He watched as she gently placed Button onto the front seat.

'Uhm, I know it's not really ice cream weather,' Nat said, 'but why don't we go for ice cream tomorrow? I was reliably informed that Beldon has a famous ice cream parlour, but I'm yet to try it,' he added.

Alana stared up at him in the cool, breezy air.

'I'd really like that,' she replied. Button was getting hungry and started barking from inside the car. 'The ice cream parlour is close to my studio - final class of the day finishes at 4:30PM. Can I meet you then?' Baxter looked at her with a puzzled expression. 'I run a ballet school,' she explained.

'Uh huh,' he replied. 'So, you're a teacher too? Wow.'

'Yes, I am, and I love it. It's so rewarding to be able to pass on all I've learned to aspiring young dancers. Alana's Dance Academy, it's a few doors down from the ice cream shop,' she said.

'Great! I'll see you tomorrow afternoon, after school,' said Nat, referencing both their careers. She giggled and gave him a 'I see what you did there' type look before getting in her car. Baxter was floating on cloud nine as he watched her drive away. Button had jumped into the back seat and was peering back at him from the rear window. He walked slowly back home with a smile etched on his face. He hadn't felt like this in some time and was elated.

The following day passed quickly, much to Nat's delight, and all he could think about was Alana. His happy day did, however, contain one blemish when he had a visit from Richard after the third period, who expressed his desire to quit learning the guitar! Nathan was astonished and dismayed that this student, who possessed so much flair and natural ability, was not receiving the expected support from his parents. *I reckon if the kid saw someone like Queen, Clapton, Aerosmith, Neil Young or the Stones live in concert, he'd see the light, stand up to his folks and never look back!* mused Nat.

Once the school bell rang, Nathan told Pip that he had to leave early. He jumped in his car and eagerly made his way to Beldon. He stopped off at a milk bar to buy a cola, hoping it would calm his nerves. It didn't, and as he neared his destination, the sight of the ice cream parlour, combined with the rush of sugar and adrenaline, only made him more anxious. Baxter parked his car outside of the Beldon newsagency and took a deep breath. He did a double-take upon noticing that, next to the newsagent, there was a boutique clothing store named 'Amber's'. The irony was not lost on Nat as he checked his hair in the mirror and ensured his shirt collar wasn't sticking up. He spat out his gum, took one final swig of cola, grabbed his jacket, and removed the key from the ignition.

'Follow your heart Baxter,' he said aloud, slamming the car door shut. As he walked towards the studio, several mother–and-daughter combinations walked past him. Most of the young girls wore tutus, which confirmed he was in the right location. Alana's Dance Academy was a white, two-story building with large windows. Twirling swans were painted on either side of the front door, while some thriving fern plants adorned the foyer. A carpeted stairway, Nat assumed, led to the ballet studio above. Alana was engaged in a conversation with a student's mother, who exited after a few minutes. The pretty teacher smiled as she escorted the lady from the studio. Alana shut the front door, flipped the *open* sign to *closed*, and turned to face Nathan.

'Hello,' she said warmly. 'It's lovely to see you again.

'It's nice to see you too,' replied Nat, who felt like he was blushing.

'I am sorry about that, Nathan,' said Alana, apologising for her lateness. 'One of my students is struggling to focus in class, and I needed to discuss it with her mother.'

'I see,' he replied. 'It's so nice that you have a good rapport with the parents. I won't go into it now, but I have one particular student who is a really gifted guitar player. He gets zero support from his parents and is talking about quitting.'

'How awful,' replied Alana, closing the blinds. 'Just let me lock up, and I'll meet you outside, OK?' Nat smiled and nodded.

He waited a few minutes, then watched as she double-checked the locked door.

'Who's looking after your cute dog, Button, today?' he asked, walking away from the building.

'That cute little guy is with my parents. Come on, the

ice cream shop is this way,' she said, pointing ahead. Baxter looked over at Alana. Whatever nerves he had felt earlier dissipated as he quickly grew more comfortable with her.

'I hope they've got jaffa,' he said, as they strolled toward the store.

'They've got 58 flavours, so I think you'll be in luck,' said Alana.

'My daughter Hanna really loves strawberry-swirl.' said Nat.

Alana stopped for a moment and looked at him quizzically.

'You have a daughter?' she asked, surprised.

'Yes, Hanna - she's nearly 8 years old, and she's the light of my life,' he said. 'She lives with her Mum, but I've recently been seeing her every fortnight.' Alana looked at him for a moment and then broke into a smile.

'I bet she's a great dancer.'

'Oh, she is!' replied Nat, smiling. 'And I'm sure she'd love ballet; I know she would.' He was a little worried about her reaction to him being a Dad, and Alana's response was a relief. They bought ice cream and walked across to the wharf, where they sat down on a bench overlooking the ocean.

'I imagine that you've danced in many famous cities. How does it feel to be back in Beldon?' asked Nat.

'It feels nice, and you're right - I've travelled and seen the lights of London, Paris, Moscow, Milan, Vienna and more, but I love it here. It's my home,' she replied. 'And just look at that beautiful skyline as dusk approaches. I wish I were a painter so I could preserve on canvas some of the exquisite sunsets I've seen from Beldon. I also find peace here,

Nathan, and that's really important to me.' Alana turned her head for a moment and looked downward, and he wondered if her comment meant anything. 'How is your jaffa ice cream?' she asked.

'It's delicious. Orange citrus and chocolate are a match made in ice cream heaven. I've loved it since I was a kid, and it's kinda hard to locate nowadays. I mean, there are some serious issues in the world, I know, and the availability of jaffa ice cream probably isn't one of them - but it should be,' he laughed. 'There, I've given you the scoop, but I will waffle on no more,' he added. She burst out laughing.

'That joke's terrible, Nathan!'

'I know, but you laughed!' he replied. 'And Alana,' he added with a more serious tone, 'please call me Nat.' She looked at him warmly and nodded. They sat on the bench talking until the sky had turned dark and cold. Nat removed his denim jacket and placed it over Alana's shoulders. Feeling hungry, she suggested fish and chips, and Baxter quickly agreed. 'Best idea I've heard all day, I am starving!'

While waiting in line for their order to be cooked, 'Already Gone' by The Eagles played over the radio. Losing all control, Baxter threw his head back in delight, grabbed Alana's hands, and started dancing, much to the dismay of other customers. Although somewhat shy, Alana laughed aloud, immersed in his joy.

'Glenn Frey sounds *amazing* on vocals, and man oh man, how *great* are those harmonies!' he hollered. A couple of customers, watching on, were now smiling at the happy couple. One of them began tapping his foot in time with the rhythm.

'Order number 84,' yelled the shop assistant, cutting short the impromptu performance. Gathering their food, Nathan and Alana exited the fish and chip shop, giggling like teenagers.

'I've never done *anything* like that before in my life,' she exclaimed.

'I didn't mean to embarrass you, Alana, but music means so much to me. It's my lifeblood and sometimes it moves me - quite literally! There is something about good rock 'n' roll that, when I hear it, just takes over me,' said Nat.

'I could see!' she replied. 'I really wish I knew more about music, and that song back there sounded so great.' Nat made a mental note to pick her up some cassettes during the week.

As it was chilly, they decided to eat dinner in the warmth of Nat's car.

'I would've cleaned up if I had known I was having a guest over,' he chuckled.

'It's fine,' replied Alana, who, no sooner after uttering that, dropped some of the oily food on the car seat! She apologised repeatedly, but Nat just laughed it off, as things like that never bothered him.

'Alana, there's no point crying over spilt milk...or spilt fish,' he chuckled. '...and 'I'll get Checkers to do a final clean up later.' Her face lit up with a warm glow when she heard his response. She didn't tell him just yet, but she had previously been engaged to another dancer - a fiancé who was very controlling with an explosive temper as well. She watched as Baxter played air guitar to a song on the radio. He seemed down-to-earth and genuine, and she felt comfortable with him. Baxter dropped Alana at her parents' house just after 8:00PM. The porch light flicked on as he pulled into their driveway, which made him smile - it was something his Mum and Dad would do. He hopped out and opened the door for her - now it was her turn to blush.

'Thanks for a wonderful afternoon, Nathan, I mean Nat. I really enjoy your company.'

'I feel the same, Alana,' he said. 'Would you like to have dinner with me on Friday night? The steaks at The Southern Anchor are mouth-watering.'

'I would love that,' she replied without hesitation. 'However, I run classes late on Fridays, but I am free on Saturday.'

'Saturday evening it is, then - let's say 7:30PM?' he asked.

'That sounds lovely, Nat. I'm already looking forward to it. Let me give you my phone number,' she said, reaching into her bag for a biro and paper. She wrote quickly in the dimly lit driveway and handed him the note. He placed it in his top pocket and then said goodbye.

'Oh my God!' he shouted once behind the wheel. 'She's incredible!' Of course, Baxter was aware he had only just met her the day before, but he trusted in his feelings - it was something he really believed in. He drove back to Clare on a high, tapping the wheel and singing at the top of his voice. After he arrived home, he cut the engine and turned on the interior light to read the note Alana had written:

Alana, 850-4179 (celui?)

Puzzled by the mystery word she'd written at the end of the sentence, he folded the piece of paper and returned it to his pocket. Checkers was sitting on the old sofa, watching him as he stepped up to the porch.

'I've had the *best* day, Check,' he said, as the cat jumped down and rubbed her body on his legs. He unlocked the front door and watched as Checkers scurried inside. After a shower, Baxter put on a thick sweater, uncapped a beer, placed *461 Ocean Boulevard* on the Hi-Fi, then headed for the porch. Checkers was curled up in a blanket on the sofa and Nat sat alongside her. She raised her head and greeted him with a soft meow. 'Well hello there, Madam,' he said, gently scratching the side of her face. She enjoyed the affection for a few seconds before returning to her sleeping position. Nathan placed his feet on the small coffee table, rested his head back, and let images of Alana dance effortlessly across his mind. It was amazing to think that only the day before, he'd been thrust back into that dark world of frustration and disappointment, and now, here he sat, floating on air - salt air at that. Who knows how the heart works and why certain people's paths cross? Nat certainly didn't, and he wasn't going to overthink things. But to meet the very lady who he'd seen and locked eyes with in Carl's car some weeks back was un-canny. He took a swig of beer and looked up at the stars.

Is it fate? Is it meant to be? he pondered. He watched as a shooting star hurtled across the crisp, clear sky. Clapton's vocals on the song 'Let It Grow' permeated through the air, filling his heart with warmth. 'God is giving me a sign,' he said, smiling. Maybe it *is* fate?

Nursing the beer bottle in one hand, he used the other to softly rub Checkers' head, all the while taking in the music. The sound of the waves eventually lulled him to sleep, but sometime around 2:00AM, he was awoken by the familiar 'click-click-click' sound, courtesy of the Hi-Fi's still broken auto-return mechanism. Baxter groaned, then got to his feet, carrying Checkers inside the house.

| 7 |

Let It Grow

Baxter slept solidly through the six o'clock alarm, but sat bolt upright and shot out of bed upon realising it was after eight! He startled Checkers, who was sound asleep, and the cat sprang onto the floor.

'Damn it!' he cursed, rushing to find some clean, presentable work clothes. Checkers blinked, watching Nat as he darted to the bathroom to splash cold water on his face, then to the wardrobe where he gathered some clothes and tossed them on the bed. As he sat down to put on his socks, Checkers began playing with his necktie, swishing at the long length of silk with kitten-like energy. 'Get outta here, ya little scamp,' he said, hauling the tie away from her and placing it around his neck. Nat then quickly made some toast, coating it with butter and honey. He cut one slice into small pieces (which he fed to Checkers), stuffed the other in his mouth, and rushed out the door. Although it was only a short drive to school, he was grateful for the car as it was raining once again. Maybe there was some truth to that slogan on the town's welcome sign? He parked his car and, with his jacket over his head, hurried into the school office. He passed Pip who playfully pointed her finger at him.

'Just in the nick of time,' she said grinning, as he headed for the music room. As he entered, all the students were perched on their chairs, nursing their guitars, awaiting his arrival. A trio of kids were huddled together, heads down, practicing chord progressions.

'Good morning, everyone,' said Nat. 'And a special hello to the three-guitar army over there,' he added, pointing at the three kids. 'Keep practicing, and you too can play like the guys in Skynyrd. But until then, let's spread out and give ourselves some room, huh?' Some kids laughed as they opened their sheet music and followed Nat's lead, as he ran through some warm-up exercises. By 10:00AM, his stomach growled for food, and, for once, he wished that one of his students had placed the customary apple on his desk to show their respect. That old cliché had never happened in his career yet, and would have to wait until another day. Baxter would also have to wait until lunch to visit the school canteen and grab something to eat.

The rain that day had set in and tapped loudly against the glass window. Not that any students in Baxter's music room would have noticed, as they were all immersed in their guitars. Although he had overslept, by mid-afternoon, Nat was feeling the effects of the late night and was pleased to see the clock tick over to 5:00PM - exit time.

He wanted to purchase some music cassettes for Alana, but the heavy rain, not to mention his heavy eyelids, persuaded him to postpone that task until tomorrow. He drove home wearily, fed Checkers some dry food, then collapsed in a hot bath. He thought about Hanna and wondered how her day was, hoping she'd had an umbrella packed in her school bag. Try as he might, parental thoughts like that never ceased, and he was OK with that. He also thought about Alana, conjuring up graceful images of her dancing at famous theatres like the Palais Garnier in Paris or the Bolshoi Theatre in Moscow. *Amazing,* he thought. *She's danced her way to the very top of the ballet world.* Baxter splashed some water on his face, then climbed out of the bath. Images of Alana continued to float through his mind as he towelled himself dry. In a moment of affection, he scrawled '*A + N*' on the foggy bathroom mirror and encircled it with a heart.

'I wonder if you're thinking about me, as I am of you?' he asked aloud, standing in front of the mirror-message. 'Come on, Baxter, you're not a teenager,' he added with a chuckle. Yet, he felt really comfortable with her and he felt so alive. It was a positive sign.

The following day at school was uneventful, except for Carl bringing in some leftover fish and calamari rings for the staff, which were quickly devoured before lunch! By the time Nat got to the staff room, the only thing remaining was the oily newspaper that had housed the meal! 'Nice,' he said sarcastically, with a half-smile. 'I'm working with some very hungry bears.' Thankfully, Pip had saved him some of the fish for which he, and his rumbling tummy, were most grateful. He owed her one.

After school, Baxter paid another visit to Clare's

Records and Tapes. Tucked away in Angela's Arcade, the tiny store with the slogan 'More Wax Than Madame Tussauds!' stocked a large variety of vinyl, cassettes, and rare items. Since arriving in the coastal town, Nat had been there several times and picked up many items for his collection. Clare was passionate about rock 'n' roll, and it made Nathan happy to talk about music with a kindred spirit. She also happened to be a huge fan of John Lennon. After Nat shared his story of bumping into John and Yoko ten years earlier, Clare's face would light up whenever he entered the store - and today was no exception. After greeting Clare with some Top 40-related small talk, Nat explained the reason for his visit, then headed for a large table packed with cassettes. Music is a personal taste, and choosing selections for someone you don't know very well can be daunting. He tapped through the tiles, pausing on something he thought Alana may dig: *The Best of Bread?* Yes. Kiss or Status Quo? Too loud. *Harvest* by Neil Young? Yes! *Broken Heart* by The Babys? Sure. *The Saturday Night Fever* soundtrack? Pass. Heart's *Dreamboat Annie?* Yes! *Creedence Gold* by Creedence Clearwater Revival? Next time. He picked up a copy of The Eagles, *Their Greatest Hits (1971–1975)* album and looked over the song titles. This led to thoughts of his impromptu dance with Alana at the Beldon fish and chip shop. Smiling, he put the cassette to one side.

'The brand new Wings album *Back To The Egg* arrived yesterday,' said Clare. 'The first single, 'Old Siam Sir,' is terrific!' she exclaimed before playing the 45 loudly over the store's speakers. Nat tapped his foot, digging the tune. 'You should get your friend a copy of *Wings Greatest*,' she shouted.

'I mean, that's what friends are for, right?' Baxter looked over and smiled at her. Maybe Clare didn't interpret an entirely accurate meaning of the quote she'd shared, but she had said it with pure intention and he agreed that it *was* an album that Alana should hear.'

'Great idea, Clare,' he replied, gathering up his collection of cassettes and taking them to the counter. 'I think these choices are pretty solid and are albums which everyone should hear.'

'You know your rock 'n' roll, Nathan, friend of the great John Lennon.' she said with a grin. After making the sale, she handed him his change and packed his albums. 'Keep on rockin', Mr. Baxter.'

'Always,' said Nathan. He winked, then exited the store, happy with his purchases.

After Clare's, he swung by Nugget's and bought half a chicken and chips for dinner before driving home. Although chilly, he sat on the porch and ate his meal, enjoying the serenity and shoreline sounds. His moment of peace was broken by the arrival of Checkers, whose powerful sense of smell detected her owner's dinner. 'I knew it wouldn't be long before you appeared,' he said laughing. Checkers sat near his feet and looked up at him longingly. He handed her some chicken pieces, which she ate quickly before jumping up on the sofa. 'Oh man, you're gonna eat all my dinner!' complained Nat. 'Come on, let's go inside, and I'll find you something else to eat.'

After dinner, Nat pocketed some coins and walked slowly to the telephone booth located at the end of Auger

Avenue. A light fog had crept over the coastal town which he found enchanting. Nat unfolded Alana's note, inserted some coins into the slot, then dialled her number. His heartbeat quickened as he listened to the ringing telephone, prompting him to take a deep breath to fend off any nerves.

'Hello,' said Alana.

Hearing her voice made him feel alive, as if a jolt of energy had surged through his body. He realised he was falling in love.

'Hi Alana, it's Nat.'

'Nat!' she replied enthusiastically. 'How are you?'

'Oh, I'm doing great. It's really nice to hear your voice.'

'Thankyou. Same here,' she said, '...and I really want to say how much I enjoyed being with you earlier this week.' He was beaming whilst tapping nervously on the adjacent telephone directory. As he listened to her talk about her day at the ballet studio, he felt himself being drawn into her world - and he liked it. He told her about Carl bringing fish to school and of his hungry colleagues, which made her laugh.

'Man, she has a cute giggle,' he thought.

'Alana, I have a surprise for you, next time I see you.' She let out a small gasp.

'That's so nice! I wonder what it is?'

'You'll see, well, you'll hear soon enough,' replied Nat, referring to his cassette gift-stack. 'I'm looking forward to dinner on Saturday night.'

'Oh, me too,' said Alana, who then paused for a moment. 'But it's you I am really looking forward to seeing.' Nat felt a warmth course through his body as he peered out from the window in the booth.

'Thankyou. That makes me feel special. I'm excited too - and not only for the steak, although it's pretty tasty!' he added. She giggled again. He made plans to pick her up from Beldon on Saturday before hanging up. He felt alive while walking back home and noted that his mouth was sore - from smiling. *A person can never smile too much,* he thought, unlocking the front door.

The rain settled in over Clare once again for the latter part of the week, making Baxter hope for an early spring arrival. Yet, that was still some weeks away. Regardless of the climate, he would settle on the porch after work and use the time to write poetry, some of which would later resurface in songs. Although Nat enjoyed the challenges of working at a new school, he was nevertheless looking forward to the up-coming school break. He was keen to spend time with Hanna, and hopefully Alana as well! Nat was also busily planning the school's annual Christmas concert, during which each class performed a song for parents and friends. But he also hit upon another idea - one that brought back the excitement he had felt as a member of his teenage outfit, The Nighthawks. So, with Carl's approval and their parents' permission, a rock band was formed to play songs beyond the confines of school. And thus, The Sea Fleas were born. Four of Nathan's most competent students made up the group, with the view to exchange members as time progressed. Baxter plugged in on second guitar, as well as taking on the role of band manager - a job which he hoped one of the parents could fill later on. Besides having copious amounts of fun and learning to play live, the project encouraged students in other classes to improve *their* chops and hopefully become a 'sea flea' too - or even start their own band!

Friday afternoon, Nat did overtime at school, then swung by Nugget's for a burger with the lot and some time on the pinnies. Since he was last in the store, two video games had arrived, which attracted a large swarm of kids. *Space Invaders* and *Galaxian?* Nat looked on as the teenage player killed off the fast-descending aliens with some rapid-fire shooting. At one point, a UFO flew across the screen and the kid took a shot at it as well. Bemused, Baxter collected his burger and chips from the counter before walking home. 'Aliens, Space Invaders, UFOs - I don't get it,' uttered the pinball-loving Baxter. 'It's not my world - and the only UFO I want flying into my world is through my speakers - with guitarist Michael Schenker on board, blasting 'Doctor Doctor' and 'Rock Bottom!' he added, referring to the loud rock 'n' roll band from London. He passed a fisherman on the wharf cleaning his catch and stopped to see what he'd caught. The angler had a good haul of tailor and offered one to Nat, who immediately thought of his furry black-and-white buddy waiting for him at home. Baxter thanked the fisherman and handed him a couple of bucks for his kindness. As he approached the porch, he sang out to his cat with his signature call - something fun which harked back to his days gigging in Gothenburg with Edvard.

'Check, check, check 1-2, yeah yeah, check, Checkers.....dinner!' hollered Nat. *The neighbours probably think I'm mad with that cat call, but who cares? Unless, of course, they're former roadies,'* he mused. His pet cat darted out from the nearby bushes and bounded onto the porch. 'You know I have something for you, don't you?' said Nat with a smirk. 'Come on, let's head into the kitchen and I'll cut up your dinner.'

Baxter lay in bed that night, thinking about Alana and just how wonderful the past week had been. 'It's meant to be.' he said aloud, moving the curtain to gaze at the stars. He was really looking forward to tomorrow night's dinner date, and, whether he realised it or not, he hadn't given Amber or her continued hostility any attention. New love is like a rising sun, and he was ready to bask in the warmth of this woman whom he sensed was his soulmate. With positive thoughts floating through his mind, he peacefully drifted off to sleep.

The following morning, Nat walked to the beach and took a dip in the icy blue water. He wasn't the world's best swimmer, but a few minutes alone with the cold ocean waves was something he found invigorating - and if that led to a positive and productive day, then even better. To build mental strength, he had once read how monks would start their day by pouring a bucket of cold water over themselves - an activity he sometimes tried to emulate. Baxter clearly did not possess the self-discipline of a monk; however, he did identify with their minimalistic and serene way of life. As an aside, he'd occasionally tell people that he attained enlightenment at that Blind Faith gig back in June of '69!

After returning from the beach, Nat drove over to Port Stafford for some much-needed grocery shopping. Larger than Clare but smaller than Beldon, Port Stafford also had an arcade centre called Tilt!, which Baxter was keen to check out! The locals affectionately called it 'Port Staffy,' a term that Nat found nauseating. He was always perplexed why people liked to abbreviate place names, and believed that it somehow diminished the character of the town. After loading his car with fruit, bread, cat food, cereal, coffee, and other groceries, Nat walked over to Tilt! to play the silver ball. As with Nugget's, the arrival of several stand-up video games was evident. However, to his delight, a variety of pin-ball machines lined the walls. He exchanged some notes for a handful of coins and surveyed the flashing machines. Ted Nugent 45s, such as 'Stranglehold' and 'Cat Scratch Fever' copped plenty of time on Baxter's Hi-Fi, so naturally, he stopped at a machine dedicated to the guitar-slinger from Detroit. He was about to roll a coin into the *Nugent* machine when his gaze shifted toward the corner of the room, and his mouth fell open. 'No way!' he exclaimed, walking over to the weathered blue and white-coloured machine that stood unloved: *Hearts and Spades*! It was a machine into which he had fed countless krona during his time in Gothenburg. He gazed at the backglass - an image of five girls holding play-ing cards, and was instantly transported back to that magic winter of 1969. The Solnedgång Tavern was within walk-ing distance of the Johanssen's home, a bar that Amber and Nathan visited regularly - and *Hearts and Spades* was one of two pinball machines located in the tavern that Baxter loved. Amber would sit on an adjacent bar stool admiring his skills, and he'd often clock the machine. On bitterly cold nights they would sit huddled together, drinking dark beer near the open fireplace, then stumble back home with their arms around each other. These images made Nat smile. Sure, he'd recently been ripped apart, but there were plenty of good times and he acknowledged that. As soon as he pulled the plunger back and shot the first ball, the memories returned back from whence they came and he focused on the game.

Later that afternoon, Baxter cranked the Stones' latest LP, *Some Girls* and cracked open a beer to ease into the evening. He ironed a shirt and tie, splashed on some *Midnight Mood* aftershave, and danced in rhythm to the song 'Respectable'. His dance moves ventured into air-guitar territory and were a hybrid mix of both Ronnie Wood and Keith Richards.

'Damn, this tune is good!' he exclaimed, gulping down the ale. So good, that he lifted the styli and returned it to the beginning of the track. He switched on his amp, swung the '59 Les Paul over his shoulder and leaned in close to the Hi-Fi speaker. Lost in the music, Baxter spent the next half hour trying to figure out the guitar solo while playing along with the song. He finished off the beer, glanced at the clock and gasped…he was now running late! Nat carefully returned the Les Paul to its guitar stand and switched off the amp. He rushed into his bedroom and grabbed his car keys and black leather jacket. He noticed Checkers asleep on the bed, so, on the way out, poured milk into her bowl and scattered some dry cat food. 'See ya,' he said, before locking the front door.

He arrived at Alana's parents' house at a quarter to eight, fifteen minutes late. Alana exited the front door and made her way down the stairs. Her father followed close behind, so Baxter stepped out of the car and introduced himself with a firm handshake.

'Nathan Baxter, it's a pleasure to meet you, sir.'
The man in his mid-60s looked into Nathan's eyes and silently

exhaled. His face was partially illuminated by the porch light, and Nat noticed that his jaw was slightly disfigured - the result of an injury, he would later explain, sustained from flying shrapnel.

'Frank Perry,' he said. 'Nice to meet you, son. Look after our daughter.'
Nathan heard the sternness in Alana's father's voice, etched in his short greeting and nodded his acknowledgment. 'She's been through a lot,' he added.

'Yes, sir, absolutely,' replied Nat, looking directly at Mr. Perry, who smiled a little. Baxter turned and walked towards Alana, who was standing beside his vehicle. He opened the door for her and glanced back at her Dad, who remained motionless.

'*She's been through a lot?*' pondered Nat, wondering what that comment could mean. He shook his head and turned to Alana, who looked stunning. 'Well hello there,' he smiled.

'Hi Nathan,' she replied softly. 'I'm *really* hungry,' she added, poking his shoulder. He tilted his head back and apologised.

'Man, I'm so sorry I'm late,' he said, watching as Mr. Perry walked unsteadily inside the house. He reminded Nat of his former co-workers from the ship chandler he had worked with a decade or so earlier. Cut from the same cloth. Baxter clicked his seat belt tight, started the car and slowly drove off. When he explained to Alana the reason *why* he was late, her eyes glistened and she burst into laughter.

'Nat, you really are one of a kind, aren't you?!' He liked it when she called him that. He looked over at her. Her hair was tied back in a ponytail, revealing a rose gold necklace that nestled around her slender neck. 'It's safe to say you're as passionate about music as I am about ballet.' They both laughed as they made their way to Clare and the Southern Anchor for dinner.

'You recently mentioned that you wished you knew more about music,' stated Nat. She looked at him quizzically. 'Miss Alana, there's a present for you in the glove box.'
She smiled, leaned forward and then lifted the latch on the compartment, revealing a rectangular-shaped object inside. Alana turned on the vehicle's interior light and inspected the gift, which was wrapped in pink paper decorated with unicorns.

'Forgive me,' he said, 'the only wrapping paper I had was left over from my daughter's birthday.'
'It's cute,' she replied. 'Funny story - I once performed in a ballet in Glasgow called *Starlight Flight*. It was a narrative ballet for kids, and the storyline centred on a unicorn named *Hope*. I played the role of another unicorn named *Purity*. The costumes were incredible Nat! I'll have to show you the program.'

'I'd love that,' he replied. 'And I get the feeling you have a pure heart, so dancing as a character named *Purity* makes perfect sense,' he blurted, the words out of his mouth before he knew it.

Alana smiled and looked lovingly at him then returned her attention to the gift. She ripped open the packaging, and, upon seeing the cassettes, giggled with joy.

'Thankyou! What a nice surprise. No one's ever

bought me cassettes before!'

'Play something,' said Nat, ejecting the current cassette from the deck. Although unaware of the artists, Alana opened one of the cassettes and slotted it into the car stereo.

'Bread, 'Make It With You'...great choice,' commented Nat as the first song began to play. 'This is *The Best Of Bread* and man, David Gates' vocals are as smooth as butter - no pun intended,' he added, referring to the band's lead singer. Baxter raised the volume and joined in on the chorus. They arrived at the Southern Anchor just as a group of visiting bowls players were exiting. A couple of the old-timers gave Alana a wolf whistle before boarding their small bus, which she laughed off. Over a mouth-watering steak dinner, Nathan chatted about his life in rock 'n' roll and regaled his beautiful date with stories of the many concerts he'd attended. She was suitably impressed that he'd once cut a 7" single and had also taken out a 'battle of the bands' competition.

'I'd really love to hear that song, 'Pristine Heart,' one day. Is that a self-reflective title?' asked Alana. He looked back at her over his wine glass. 'You mentioned earlier that *Purity* the unicorn and I shared a warm heart. I haven't known you for very long, Nat, but I can already sense that you, too, have a heart that is pure.' They stared at each other for a brief moment before she looked away, blushing a little. He smiled and felt a warmth wash over him.

'How did you come up with that band name, The Nighthawks ?' she asked, breaking the silence. Nat thought for a moment before replying.

'Our bass player suggested it after claiming he saw a

hawk sitting on a phone line while walking home from band practice. Thinking back, he wasn't much of a birdwatcher, we were city kids - and we'd all had a couple of beers that night, so in all reality, it might as well have been a sparrow or pigeon he saw! But the name fit so we kept it.' They both laughed loudly.

During their conversations, he skirted around his divorce but did share fond memories of Hanna's early years - like when she first learned to walk, or the time they went fishing when she was a toddler, and she cleverly washed her dummy in the water after dropping it on the sand. In the back of his mind, Nathan secretly hoped that, if this relationship moved forward, that Hanna and Alana could form a strong bond. That would take time, but it was already important enough to be on his mind. After dinner, they decided to skip dessert, and headed to the nearby Seahorse Inn for a drink.

'Irasshaimase. Konbanwa, Nathan-san,' said Noriko with an enthusiastic wave, greeting him in Japanese from behind the bar. Baxter smiled and found a quiet window table, pulling out the seat for Alana. Charli took their order and returned with some drinks a short while later. Apart from the regular barflies and a couple of loud drunks playing pool, the place was unusually quiet for a Saturday evening. Half-way through his dai-jockey Baxter's face lit up.

'Come on, let's dance!' he suggested, grabbing Alana's hand and leading her towards the small dance floor near the jukebox.

'Choose something modern, Mr. Baxter,' teased Charli as he leaned over the jukebox. Baxter jokingly poked his tongue out at her, then queued up Journey's 'Wheel In The

Sky' followed by Fleetwood Mac's 'Rhiannon' - something he thought Alana might find appealing. He returned to the dance floor and rejoined his date, who had let her long hair down and was moving in time with the music. Baxter's dance moves were limited, and she obviously had the flair of a world-class dancer; anyone could see that. Her hairband was now secured to her wrist and Alana glided freely from side to side. He watched in awe as she danced effortlessly around him. With her long hair, high cheekbones and cute nose, she could have been channelling Stevie Nicks from Fleetwood Mac - only Alana had no idea who she was. As they continued dancing in time with the music, their eyes locked, and they felt as if they were floating. Nathan felt really comfortable in her company and was smitten.

'I saw Fleetwood Mac, late '69 in Gothenburg,' he said, leaning in close to her ear. 'Different line-up from this one, though, and they were amazing!' Alana politely smiled and nodded, just as one of the drunks who'd been playing pool suddenly strutted onto the dance floor and got in Nathan's face.

'You're that fancy music teacher, Baxter, aren't ya?' he sprayed. Nat glared at him and then glanced back at Alana, who had backed away, frightened. The guy was a little shorter than Nathan, around 40 years old, overweight, with a thick black beard. He wore a black and red check flannel under denim overalls and reeked of fish. Actually, it was a combination of fish, beer, and tobacco.

'Do I know you, brother?' asked Nat.

The drunk pushed a finger into Nat's chest and grinned.

'You think you're better than me because you're a teacher,' he sneered.

'Hey! We don't want no trouble here or I'll call the cops,' shouted Noriko from the bar. Nat took a step back, held out his hands, and once again asked the drunk how he knew him.

'You must think you're Chuck Barry or someone?' slurred the fisherman, glancing at his friend who was leaning on the pool table. His pool-playing pal, equally hammered, nodded and gave a supportive chuckle.

'Actually, it's Berry, not Barry, and I in fact worship Chuck, who is one of the greats,' replied Nat. The drunk's face turned crimson as he continued to stare down Baxter. 'You know what?' said Nathan, walking towards Alana who had placed herself near the jukebox. 'Some Chuck sounds like a great idea. I don't mind if I do.' Nathan then rolled a coin into the machine, pressed the required letter/number combination, and within seconds, the distinctive opening riff of Chuck Berry's 'School Days' blared loudly from the speakers. Nat took Alana's hand and resumed dancing, much to the annoyance of the angry drunk who stood seething on the edge of the dance floor. He waited until the completion of the song before resuming the harassment.

'My kid's in your music class, Baxter, and I'm tired of you shoving the guitar down his throat…making trouble for my family!' he said.

'Hey Monty, it's time we left.' yelled his friend from the pool table. In a flash, Baxter quickly put two and two together. This blitzed buffoon's nickname was *Monty*, no doubt short for Montgomery - Richard's Dad.

'Look, I'm not sure what your beef is with me, Mr. Montgomery. But I'm sure we can work it out, and brother, a fist-fight's not the answer. Because no matter who wins, we're both gonna get hurt, and the only one who'll lose out is your son Richard - who I've got a lot of time for and who has a wonderful future ahead of him.' This comment seemed to jolt Mr. Montgomery, who stood silent for a few moments before replying.

'The Montgomerys have been farming oysters for generations. My father was an oyster farmer, and his Dad was too. Young Richard's gonna carry on that tradition because it's who we are. He's an oyster farmer, *not* a guitar player,' he barked.

'Brother, it's your call, but your kid has talent, and wasted talent is like watching a diamond turn to dust. The guitar can shape your son's life if you'd just allow him the freedom to nurture his gift. Have you even heard him play?'

Mr. Montgomery gazed down at his muddy shoes.

'I thought so,' said Nat. 'Look, let's not discuss this here. How about I buy you a beer to show there are no hard feelings? Maybe you and your wife could stop by the school one day this week to hear Richard play and then judge for yourselves.' Mr. Montgomery's shoulders dropped, and after a brief moment, he shook Baxter's outstretched hand. He then sat with Nathan and Alana, chatting over a beer until his friend, growing tired of playing pinball, suggested they leave. The mood was a lot calmer with the departure of the two blind ocean otters - and once they were out of the pub, Charli thanked Nat for sorting out the two 'hammered hammer-heads.'

'Hey, I like that!' said Nat, referring to her catchy description of Montgomery and his mate. She grinned. After sharing a large glass of Irish cream, Baxter noticed it was past midnight and that he had to get Alana home. They bid farewell to Charli and Noriko then exited The Seahorse Inn. A fresh breeze greeted them as they walked towards his car, and Nat pointed out a constellation of stars that were visible. When he was a kid, he had been fascinated by the night sky. He found it enchanting and would sometimes lie on the soft grass, gazing up in wonder…..that is, until his mother realised he wasn't in bed and would holler at him to come in from the garden! In what could be described as a 'loud whisper' she would keep her voice low so as not to alert the neighbours. He smiled at the memory.

'What are you smiling about?' Alana asked.

'Star-gazing on school nights,' he replied. 'Hey, why don't we quickly visit the wharf? Sometimes, the starlight is really bright down there, and it creates a wonderful atmo-sphere.'

Alana agreed. Feeling cold, she folded her arms for warmth, and Baxter removed his leather jacket, placing it over her shoulders.

'Nathan, that was amazing what you did back there,' she said, walking alongside him. 'You not only managed to defuse and calm that man but also built some rapport with him too.' She stopped and looked up at him. 'I really like how you resolved that incident in a nonviolent way. Peace, love and harmony are the only things I need in my life right now.'

He smiled.

The wind had picked up, blowing her hair into her face, which he removed. They leaned in close and embraced on the creaking wharf.

'I have to confess, though, that I *can* often attack my guitar quite violently during an emotion-charged solo.' She giggled and watched as he playfully strummed an air-guitar to emphasise the point. The lapping waves grew stronger, with one lashing against the wharf so hard that it soaked them in sea spray. 'Oh no!' cried Nat. They both laughed at the situation and hurriedly returned to his car. He placed a blanket over her and cranked the vehicle's heater as they drove back to Beldon. The porch light was on, and he escorted her to the front door, carrying her cassettes.

She turned to him and spoke softly.

'Thankyou for a really wonderful evening, Nat. I feel so happy that I met you.' He started to blush a little before replying but was lost for words.

'You can keep the blanket if you wish; I've got another one,' he said, finally finding his voice. She smiled, noting his embarrassment.

'Plant one,' she said, asking for a kiss. He leaned in and kissed her softly on her lips. She opened her sparkling eyes and warmly hugged him. Baxter jumped in his car and drove home to Clare on a high.

He felt like he had known Alana forever.

| 8 |

Broken Ballerina

Baxter awoke late on Sunday morning to heavy rain on the roof. He pulled the blankets up and snoozed - that is, until Checkers jumped up on the bed and stirred him. She followed him to the kitchen where he poured her some hot milk. He made himself a hot cup of tea and then sat out on the porch enjoying the tranquillity of the falling rain. Still licking her lips from the milk, Checkers settled herself next to him and burrowed into the blanket. He felt at peace and he loved it.

Later that afternoon, he walked to the milk bar and bought a newspaper, a can of cola, some wine gums, and a large bag of salt and vinegar chips. Chewing on the gums brought back memories of London, where he first encountered the tasty sweet. Nat stopped off at the phone box, placing the snacks and paper on a small shelf. He used his index finger to remove wine gum remnants stuck to his back teeth before reaching into his pocket for a coin. After calling Amber to confirm Hanna's upcoming school holiday arrangements, he spent the rest of the afternoon nestled on the porch with his acoustic guitar. The previous evening, Noriko had asked Nathan if he would like to start performing some solo shows at the Seahorse, to which he happily agreed. Coincidentally, it had now been ten years since he'd performed those acoustic gigs with Edvard at The Avondet in Gothenburg. The urge to play live was still there, yet he needed to get his chops up and a rainy afternoon was the ideal time to start. He rounded out the day by downing a cold bottle of Ashton Ale while cranking Bob Dylan's 1974 album *Desire.* He only got up to change sides and later placed Yvonne's Elliman's debut LP on the turntable. Nat swigged from the bottle, then leaned back, absorbing the sweet vocals of Elliman. He shut his eyes and relaxed, captivated by her interpretation of Blind Faith's 'Can't Find My Way Home.'

There was one week left before the end of school term and Nat was looking forward to the break. He was planning to spend the second week of the holidays with Hanna, who hadn't yet seen her dad's coastal home *or* met Checkers either! Although it was drizzling, Nat walked to school in the rain, clutching a large umbrella. There was something about the rain in Clare which he loved. Sure, there was that old cliché about it washing away one's troubles and being good for the garden, but for Nathan Baxter - it held a powerful and soothing effect. He did however carry a spare pair of shoes in his bag, just in case he happened to step in any troublesome puddles!

When he arrived in the staff room, he was greeted by a large box of iced donuts. Carl walked past with a coffee in one hand, a donut in the other and gave Nat a broad grin. He noted the look of confusion on his music teacher's face and explained that the tasty treats were a gift from a parent whose son had won the game for the Stingrays last Saturday. It was their way of celebrating, and to also thank Coach Carl for his efforts.

'Nice work, boss,' said Nat, who had once again skipped breakfast. 'This is the kinda thing that should be introduced on a weekly basis,' he added. Carl laughed as Baxter selected a donut. He poured a coffee and headed to the music room, snagging a second donut on his way out. On his desk was a dirty, white envelope that was addressed to: *Mr. Baxter - music teacher.*

Nathan placed the donut and coffee down then slit open the envelope with a biro. Inside was a note that read:

Thankyou for bringing to our attention our son Richard's musical ability. He has expressed to us his desire to learn the guitar, and we will support him in any way we can. We look forward to meeting you and discussing this further on Tuesday...Sincerely, Wayne and Anne Montgomery

Nat looked up to see a radiant Richard, smiling at him from the back of the room. Baxter nodded and returned the smile. Now that the kid had the backing of his parents, Nathan was excited about the rock 'n' roll road that could lie ahead for his student - and if Richard *did* get accepted into the *National Academy of Music,* then Nathan would have to devise a teaching plan to cater for him. He racked his musical brain whilst gazing at his student, thinking of a suitable song - and like magic, it appeared! 'Classical Gas' - the instrumental piece by Mason Williams!

'Of course,' thought Nat. Now *that* song's gonna be a challenge for Richard! He scrawled the song title on a notepad and then commenced his first class of the day. By the time lunch rolled around, Nat was feeling tired and was glad to enter the staff room for a break. He noticed Pip working on a crossword puzzle, so after making coffee, sat down next to her on the sofa.

'Mr. Baxter,' she said, smiling. 'You're just the person I need to see; Swedish city, five letters, ending with the letter 'o'. Any ideas?' she asked, tapping her biro against the newspaper then glancing at him over her reading glasses. Nat closed his eyes for a moment to focus.

'Malmö,' he replied. '...and don't forget to include the umlaut.'

'Perfect!' replied Pip. 'That fits.' Baxter smiled at her, then took a sip of coffee before resting his head back.

'I ate some of the most delicious pancakes I've ever tasted in Malmö. Just incredible,' he added. She kept working away at her puzzle as he spoke. 'I can still recall the smell when I walked into that restaurant, and oh man, they were so light and fluffy. I'd never tasted anything like it, Pip...I just totally...flipped!' He broke into a loud fit of laughter. 'You geddit ? Flipped,' he asked, grinning. She looked up at him with a blank expression. 'No?' he asked again, hoping for the slightest reaction to his gag. She pushed out her lower lip and playfully pinched her nose, indicating that his attempted joke was a stinker. The thought of hot pancakes, however, had made him even hungrier, and his often rumbling stomach complained loudly. Somewhat deflated, he excused himself, then headed to the canteen to buy some lunch.

'Hey Nathan,' said Pip from across the room. 'Maybe you'd batter think up some new jokes.' Surprised, Baxter did an about-face and started laughing at Pip's unexpected wise-crack. She gave him a cheeky wink as he exited the staff room.

Pip was still on the sofa when he returned with a sandwich fifteen minutes later.

'I thought you'd be done with that puzzle by now,' he teased. Pip cheekily poked her tongue out and shook her head.

'Luckily, I'm surrounded by knowledgeable teachers who can make the task easier,' she replied with a smirk. Baxter unwrapped his sandwich and washed down a bite with a sip of chocolate milk. His morning music classes had been fine; however, the noise emanating from an unruly drama class nearby had brought on a migraine. The irony wasn't lost on him, given that his classes were probably the noisiest in the entire school! Nevertheless, enjoying lunch on the comfy staff room sofa was a welcome moment of peace. A light tap on the shoulder from Pip nabbed his attention.

'My sister saw you at the Seahorse on Saturday night.'

'Really?' replied Nat. 'She should've said 'hello'. It was an unforgettable evening, that's for sure - in more ways than one.'

Pip looked at him for a moment before continuing.

'I don't mean to pry into your private life, Nat, but my

sister told me you were with someone, and…'

Nathan grinned at Pip and held up his hand, stopping her mid-sentence.

'It's OK; I know how gossip runs rampant around a small town, so let me explain. Alana is someone I met quite recently who I'm really fond of. She's becoming very special to me.'

Pip paused once again, this time doodling aimlessly on the newspaper.

'She's the ballerina from Beldon who made it really big, isn't she?' she asked.

This comment immediately got Baxter's attention. He nodded, amazed, but not surprised at how everyone in Clare seemed to know everyone else's business.

'Yes, that's her - Alana,' he replied. 'The ballerina from Beldon. No wait, the Beldon ballerina. They're both great song titles! Do you know her?'

'Many people on the coast know of her and the success she's had. I mean, she went from Beldon to the biggest stages in the world. We all followed her story…her journey, and the local newspaper gave her lots of coverage,' explained Pip.

Nathan smiled upon hearing all of this.

'There were stories at the time about her being with a boyfriend or husband who was really violent, used to knock her about. I'm not sure if they're true.' The smile on Baxter's face quickly vanished upon hearing this. He stood up, walked over to the window, and watched as some kids noisily en-gaged in a game of handball. He was quiet, trying to digest Pip's story when that comment from Alana's father came hurtling back at him.

She's been through a lot, he had said. Nat mulled over this comment. *She's been through a lot.*

'Are you OK?' asked Pip, her question derailing his train of thought.

'Sure, I was just thinking about what you said.'

'Please be careful, Nat. I know you've been through a lot yourself in recent times. The last thing you need is trouble with someone's ex,' finished Pip, not once taking her eyes off the crossword. Nat smiled, warmed by his colleague's genuine concern for him.

'Thanks, Mum,' he said playfully, making her look up. She gazed at him and smiled shyly.

'This isn't a big town, and in this school, the staff are like family to me. I care about each and every one of them.'

'I know you do, Pip, and I appreciate your concern,' Nat gave her a hug, then carried the remainder of his lunch back to the music room. He sat back in his chair, looked over at the row of acoustic guitars, and deliberately pushed Pip's comment to the back of his mind. He nodded to a couple of students who, eager to practice, entered the class ahead of schedule. Baxter loved the last week of school before a vacation, because the atmosphere around the place buzzed with excitement. Clare High was no different from any of the other schools Nat had worked at, as most students were keen for a couple of weeks' break to unwind. After making a sea change that involved a new employer, Baxter, too, was looking forward to some downtime and was excited about spending time with Hanna. He missed his daughter terribly, and although he tried to reason that this situation wouldn't last forever, it did little to quell waves of despair that would sometimes wash over him. There are no winners in divorce, and many children, whose worlds are turned upside down, have no say in the matter. They never asked for it. Baxter often grappled with guilt, trading off the daily experience of watching Hanna grow - for that of his own pursuit of happiness. It was unfair.

Just how did our matrimony evolve into acrimony? he thought.

Nat's attention was rattled by more of his students noisily entering the classroom. He then began the afternoon's lessons. After completing some overdue paperwork, Baxter exited the school around 6:00PM.

The rain had passed, and the air was crisp and clean. He hummed the Rainbow song 'Man On The Silver Mountain' as he walked, using his umbrella as both a walking cane and makeshift guitar. Lost in his private rock 'n' roll fantasy, he channelled the spirit of guitarist Ritchie Blackmore, feeling his spirit surge with the melody. For that brief moment in time, Baxter stood stage left at London's Hammersmith Odeon, and watched as his fretting hand grasped the neck of a white Fender Stratocaster. He looked at vocalist Ronnie James Dio who smiled back at him. Suddenly, the sound of a loud car horn snapped him back to reality. Nat glanced up to see a blue TR6 drive past. Baxter raised the umbrella and bowed - laughing aloud upon realising it was Carl who had sprung him mid-solo!

As he walked the remainder of the way home, the sound of waves from the nearby shoreline blended with the fading light and comforted him. He loved this. *The harmony that nature provides is there for all to see. However, many cannot see past their TV screens,* thought Nat, as he gazed through some open curtains. It was dinner time, and the aroma of grilled meat wafted from kitchen windows. It reminded him that he was out of cat food, and his black-and-white sidekick would soon be hungry. Sure enough, as he turned the corner onto Auger Avenue, he spotted Checkers sitting upright on the porch, waiting patiently for him. After changing into some comfortable clothes, Nat set off for the milk bar to grab some food, with Checkers following close behind. After a few metres, Nat smiled, picked her up, and carried her into the store, much to the amusement of both the owner and a fellow customer.

He saw out the remainder of the evening by sitting on the porch with his acoustic guitar, strumming through some of his favourite tunes until the sea breeze turned cool, and then he called it a night.

The following day pretty much mirrored the previous one, sans the tasty donuts which were a one-off. Richard's folks kept their word and stopped by the music room to discuss their son, with Pip delivering some coffee to help welcome them. After some initial small talk, Nat let the music do the talking. He sat back as Richard ran through Bob Dylan's 'Forever Young,' followed by a stripped-back take of The Eagles' 'Hotel California,' which Nat also sat in on. This had the desired effect, as Mr. and Mrs. Montgomery sat spellbound.

'We had no idea,' said his mother proudly, standing to

hug her son.

'That's just some of what I've learned,' beamed Richard. 'Mr. Baxter has also asked me to learn a famous song called 'Classical Gas', which is really tough, but I think I can do it.'

'You'll ace it, buddy,' said Nat, glancing at his student. Mr. Montgomery shifted uneasily in his seat, unsure of where to look or what to say. Baxter noticed him blush when Richard's voice kicked in on the chorus of the Dylan number. If he was proud of his son, his wounded pride prevented him from expressing it. Baxter felt that the meeting went well, and Richard's parents were now six-string believers. Now aware of their son's gift, they were also supportive of Nathan's plan to apply to the *National Academy of Music,* in the hope that Richard would be accepted. Nat watched them proudly hug their son.

The smile that Richard gave his teacher as he exited the room filled Baxter with pride. Sure, his profession centred on teaching music to students, but being able to spot and then nurture a student with genuine talent? Man, that's really what it was all about. Baxter had never forgotten the impact that rock 'n' roll had had on him as a teenager, and the fire still burned brightly within.

'..and Richard,' he blurted. 'Don't forget, The Sea Fleas have band practice during the school holidays.' The student turned to his teacher with a slightly determined look on his face.

'Mr. Baxter, please call me Rick,' he replied.

Nat nodded his acknowledgement. Riding on the support of his parents and the newfound confidence it brought, the budding musician had recently decided on a name change and was now calling himself Rick.

 After locking up his classroom, Nat farewelled Pip, jumped in his car, and made his way home.

As usual, there was very little to eat in his kitchen, so a stop-off at Paradise Pizza seemed like an excellent idea. While waiting for his bacon, ham, and mushroom pizza to be cooked, he grabbed a cola from the refrigerator and called Alana from the pay phone. No answer.

Hmmm, she's probably still tied up at her dance studio, he thought.

Adding garlic bread to his order, Nat paid for his meal then exited the store. After feeding Checkers, he lit some incense, opened a notebook and set up his microphone. His first solo gig at the Seahorse was on Friday night and he needed to work on a set-list. Although Noriko had mentioned a couple of acoustic sets, his current mood yearned for something a little louder. After carefully tuning his '59 Les Paul, he uncoiled the cable and plugged into his Marshall. He then unpacked and connected his talk box effect, a device he'd bought two years ago after hearing Peter Frampton use one on his *Frampton Comes Alive* album. Nat secured the device's plastic tube to his microphone and took a big swig of cola. He wiped his mouth and glanced over at Checkers, who was sitting on the sofa with her paws tucked under herself.

'You ready?' asked Nat. The cat looked back at him nonchalantly, then sleepily put her head down. Unlike most pets, Checkers was not frightened of loud guitars, having been exposed to them for some time. This led to Nat to sometimes refer to her as the 'rock 'n' roll feline'. Baxter raised his plectrum and struck down hard on the opening chord of Joe Walsh's 1973 tune, 'Rocky Mountain Way'. He immediately felt the groove of the song pulse through him as he shut his eyes and played Walsh's riffs note for note. Just as he mouthed the plastic tube and began the talk box part of the song, Checkers alerted him to someone at the front door. Nat lowered the volume, powered off the amp and unplugged the guitar. He hungrily stuffed some garlic bread into his mouth and went to the front door to investigate.

It was Alana.

'Well hi! Now this is a nice surprise,' he said excitedly, adjusting the Les Paul to give her a tight hug. She smiled shyly.

'I really wanted to see you,' said Alana quietly.

'Come on through,' said Nat, leading her into the lounge room. Alana was surprised to see an assortment of musical equipment set up and marvelled at it all. Acoustic and electric guitars, effects pedals, Marshall cabinets, a four-track recorder, and lengthy cables which snaked around the floor. Against one wall sat a Hi-Fi, and on an adjacent shelf, there was a large collection of LPs. A large poster of Eric Clapton, guitar in hand, was pinned to the wall above the Hi-Fi. Nat moved some clothes and a guitar tablature book from the sofa, and gestured for Alana to sit down. Checkers greeted Alana with a meow before affectionately nuzzling up next to her. 'That's Checkers, and I think she already likes you,' said Nat. Alana rubbed her fingers against Checkers' head and smiled as the cat purred her appreciation.

'Do your neighbours mind the noise?'

'The house next door is empty, and, as fate would have it, the guy on the other side, Mickey-Rails, is a former roadie, and he's cool,' answered Nat, plugging his guitar back in.

'By the way, you sounded great.' she said.

'Thankyou, madam. As you know, Noriko has asked me to perform some solo acoustic gigs at the Seahorse starting this Friday, so I gotta get my chops up! Let me pick up where I left off.' This time, however, he powered on the Hi-Fi and played along with the record. Alana bobbed her head in time with the music, amazed at Baxter's guitar playing. After the song was finished, he switched guitars and settled in close to the mic. He closed his eyes for a moment to focus, then began playing the intro to The Who's 'Behind Blue Eyes,' the picking pattern and lyrics capturing Alana's attention. Seeing how much the kids at school dug it when he recently played it, Nat was inspired to nail a good version and make room for it in the Seahorse set-list. While he didn't have the vocal prowess of Roger Daltrey, he'd always been able to hold a tune, and 'Behind Blue Eyes' was within his range. Nathan poured a lot of emotion into his lounge room performance, and when he looked over at Alana, she was teary-eyed.

'Hey, I didn't mean to make you cry,' he said tenderly.

'That was really beautiful,' said Alana, her breath shuddering a little as she spoke.

He handed her a small box of tissues, then sat down and put his arms around her. They stayed that way for what seemed like forever - lingering in the love that was beginning to envelope them. It was an embrace which held more significance than both of them knew.

Baxter reheated the pizza and bread in the oven,

grabbed a couple of beers, and they moved out to the porch. He lit a candle, placed a blanket over her, and then gazed skyward. Wispy clouds had gathered around a half-moon that sat high above the horizon.

'It's really relaxing out here,' said Alana. Nat looked at her, once again feeling a sense of comfort.

'The moon has a calming effect; it helps me find peace,' he replied. She stared at him for the longest time - a look filled with both love and wonder.

'The half-moon is also a yoga position that I sometimes use as a warm-up - a posture that really tests your balance.'

'Life is all about balance,' he said quietly. 'Many people at this moment are wedged on their sofa, mesmerised by the television screen. It's sad. The moon is truly beautiful. If more people took a few minutes at the end of each day to look up at the moon and stars, maybe, just maybe, it could be a positive influence and help make the world a more peaceful place. I dunno, maybe I'm a dreamer,' he said. She stood up with the blanket draped over her shoulders and walked toward him.

'Dreamer or not, I love who you are, and finding you...is a dream come true.'

She looked up at him, and he gently moved the hair from her eyes. He pulled her close to him and they kissed softly. It was warm, unhurried and tender. As he moved his head, the flowery aroma of her hair filled him with excitement. It was an exhilarating sensation he hadn't felt since meeting Amber back in Gothenburg. They looked at each other and smiled, both aware of the fire burning within their hearts. Now it was Alana who pulled him in close, reaching her arms around his neck. They held each other tight, accompanied only by the sound of the lapping waves nearby. Alana held his hand and placed it on her cheek, finding comfort in the warmth of Nat's open palm.

'I'm aware we haven't known each other long, but I sometimes think that meeting you was a dream and that I will wake up from it,' she said. Baxter took her finger and playfully poked his face with it.

'Nope, I'm real,' he replied, pressing hard into his cheek. Her eyes remained fixed on his, but her shoulders dropped a little.

'You seem so wonderful. You're a great teacher and a loving Dad. You're thoughtful, gentle, caring, soft, and have a simplistic and peaceful way that attracts me to you, but...' She looked over his shoulder at a nearby streetlight, and he took a long swig of beer.

'But what?' he asked. 'What are you trying to tell me?' She hugged Nat again and looked up at him, taking a small breath before speaking.

'I was previously engaged, but I broke it off. That relationship has left me scarred in more ways than one, and I'm really apprehensive - I'm nervous, and...oh, I don't know,' she added, looking downward, unsure of what to say. 'Can we go inside and talk?'

Baxter gave her a warm, secure embrace, and they returned to the sofa, where Checkers was sprawled out on one end. He brewed some coffee and they spoke well into the early hours. Alana was fidgety at first, but she eventually opened up and bared her soul to Nat, sharing stories about her broken engagement. Turns out that Pip's staff room chat had some truth to it. Alana's former fiancé was a fellow dancer named Brad, who had, both on stage and off, swept her off her feet. Yet, over time, the respect and warmth he had initially shown had been replaced by intimidation, anger, and violence. He was also a control freak, meaning it was his way or no way. Over time, Alana had completely fitted into Brad's shape, agreeing to his demands and ultimately losing sight of the person she once was. Nathan sat quietly, absorbing her story. He shifted uncomfortably upon hearing about the time Brad had smacked her hard enough in the mouth to knock two of her teeth out. Coward. Frank Perry's recent comments came flooding back....

'Look after our daughter,' and, *'She's been through a lot.'* was what he had said. Nat thought about this for a moment and finally connected the dots - her Dad was referring to Alana's tumultuous engagement. Lost in thought, he caught the tail-end of Alana's sentence before she got to her feet and stretched. Baxter didn't press Alana for any further information. If she wanted to reveal more details, then she would do so in her own time.

'Come here,' she said, looking up at his smiling face. 'I'm growing quite fond of you, Mr. Baxter.'

'Likewise,' said Nat. They kissed passionately and he could feel her heartbeat against his chest. She gently pulled away and looked at him once more.

'Thankyou for listening, Nat. I feel better after talking to you.'

'You got it,' he replied.

Nat walked Alana to her car and watched as she drove

away. He folded his arms for warmth, while her red tail lights blurred from view. It was three thirty.

| 9 |

Chasing Rainbows

Miraculously, he just made it to school on time the next morning. Nat had Checkers to thank for that, as her persistent meowing to be let out of the house had snapped him from his slumber. He found himself yawning throughout most of the day, but the excitement of his upcoming Friday night gig at the Seahorse kept him moving and focused. It was the perfect way to close out his first term at Clare High. He was also very much looking forward to seeing Hanna the following week, which was of course the real highlight.

He hadn't performed on stage in front of a live audience in some time and was keen to reacquaint himself with the live environment. Really, though, standing in front of students in the classroom was just an extension of playing guitar on stage, something he'd been doing since his teenage years. That's not to say he didn't have any nerves about his first gig back - he did, but if he had any butterflies in his tummy, they were tiny ones. On a couple of occasions,

Håkansson and Baxter had backed up a female singer named Annika Lindström. The young woman would often be overcome by stage fright, and Nathan would see her in the small dressing room before the show, breathing deeply and chanting a mantra….'inga fjärilar, inga fjärilar, inga fjärilar', she'd whisper. Edvard explained that it meant 'no butterflies'. For good luck, he whispered the very same mantra as he pulled up at the Seahorse. As it turned out, any feelings of apprehension dissipated when he sat down on a barstool and adjusted the microphone to his height. This was a joyous and wonderful feeling that he'd really missed. He began the set with a take of Neil Young's 'Heart of Gold,' followed by America's 'Ventura Highway.' The response to these first two numbers from the Seahorse's regular clientele was appreciative and somewhat rowdy, strengthening Baxter's confidence. He decided to play things safe for his first show back, sticking to the more commercial-sounding covers; apart from a solid take of 'Celluloid Heroes' by The Kinks which he threw in for good measure. Nat also acknowledged a couple of drunken requests for Dylan tunes - not unexpected as rapport quickly builds in those intimate gigs. What was not expected, however, was Alana walking into the tavern halfway through Nat's set. Turning heads with her long flowing hair, and pink cashmere sweater-black jeans attire, Nat's eyes followed her as she strolled to the bar, then settled at an empty table with a drink. They shot each other a tender glance as he sang and strummed his guitar.

'Another unannounced surprise,' he said, kissing her on the cheek during a break in his set. She looked up at him and smiled. Her smile was warm and pure and it made him melt. It was a warmth that filled his entire body and again, that's when he knew…he just knew. After a few minutes, Noriko glanced over at him, and he got to his feet.

'Can you please play me a Rod Stewart song?' asked Alana. 'I think it's called 'Mandolin Wind.'' Nathan did a double-take and grinned, not only because he *adored* those early '70s Rod records, but because Alana requesting a track like 'Mandolin Wind,' had likely meant that she'd searched it out. She was tapping on his musical heart and he was happy to let her in.

'Every picture tells a story,' he replied. Although his name-checking of the album from which 'Mandolin Wind' was lifted meant nothing to her, she nodded and smiled nonetheless. He returned to the small stage area and resettled on his stool. He looked over at Alana, who nursed another drink and watched him in anticipation. 'That's one pretty picture that *doesn't* tell the whole story,' he mused.

By the time the Seahorse shut its doors at 3:00AM, Baxter was beat. Alana had classes early the following day, so didn't see out all of Nat's set. As he loaded his gear into the back seat of his car, Nat heard Noriko shout her appreciation in his direction. He pulled the car door shut and sat behind the driver's wheel. Resting his weary head, he grinned and let out a little sigh of relief. It felt great to be back on stage once again.

Nat slept through most of the Saturday, surfacing only once to feed Checkers, and by late afternoon, any lingering post-gig weariness had vanished. Pulling aside the bedroom curtain, he noticed daylight slipping away, so decided to get outside for a refreshing blast of salt air. He snatched a beer from the fridge, tucked a book into his back pocket and headed for the beach. A musk-pink sky hung above the dark ocean, and Baxter stood upright, looking out to sea. He scanned over the painted sky, taking it all in. The wind whipped sand against his legs, while above, shrieking seagulls balanced in the breezy air. He inhaled deeply, and a lovely vision of Alana appeared. The image flashed and didn't linger for long, yet he clearly felt something powerful flow through him. In that moment, he had never seen more clearly, and he knew he had experienced a glimpse into the future.

He sat down on the sand, opened the book, and took a long swig of ale. He looked out to sea and could just make out the lights of a tanker far on the horizon. Baxter gulped down another mouthful, put his head back and let his mind run free. He thought of Alana, but also of Hanna and his ex-wife, Amber. There was no doubt that his recent divorce had been nasty and downright draining, yet Baxter was determined not to harbour resentment and to keep his heart free from acrimony. A person who carries love in their heart is a person who brings peace. He had always sought friendship with Amber and couldn't comprehend why they couldn't have parted as friends, especially considering how much they had shared. He had offered her an amicable parting and viewed the bitterness of their divorce, along with the accompanying exhaustion, unnecessary. What were the lyrics to Lennon's 'Imagine'? Melancholy washed over him like the nearby waves as memories continued to flow, and the good times reappeared - the early days in Gothenburg, shared meals with the Johanssen family, cradling a newborn Hanna in hospital, and looking into her eyes for the very first time. He smiled at the vision of the brick letterbox he had built with his daughter, her first day at school, walking with her on his shoulders, and how she liked to stand on a chair to soapily wash the dishes. His smile widened, and Nat could almost smell the tasty cakes that Amber used to bake as well.

'A bitter end will often sour the sweetest memories,' he mused with pursed lips. He thought back to the day his ex-wife had left him, finding the heart-shaped necklace he'd given her hanging on a hook near his toothbrush. There was no wedding band; she'd thrown that at him some time beforehand. He noted that she had kept the more valuable diamond engagement ring though. Money, the root of all evil, and if divorce had taught him one thing - it was that money did not make you happy. He and Alana had been financially secure, but what was the point if underlying issues were not addressed and allowed to fester? If you couldn't be yourself? Like many marriages, there would be long periods of happiness shattered by loud arguments. So much of their marriage revolved around doing things her way, so in order to avoid Amber's temper, he found it easier to comply. Yet, in doing so, he had ultimately lost sight of the person he once was. How the hell had he let that happen? Despite feeling immeasurable love for his daughter, fitting into someone else's shape had become an issue. How long could he have ignored it? He yearned to be truly happy, yet didn't want to make waves or impact Hanna's happiness. She was still so little. This predicament would tick away until it inevitably exploded.

He took several more gulps from the bottle.

Baxter then thought of the judge and the lawyers making decisions about his life - of the dad-and-daughter time those leeches had sucked away from him. Dark days, and a period where he'd never been so confused and unhappy in his life. But then along comes Clare, and with it, Alana - both of whom helped him rediscover himself. He wiped a tear away from his cheek, sniffed, and finished off the beer. Trying to clear his head a little, he then stood up and made his way home.

To lift his spirits, he ripped open another beer and hauled out his copy of the Stooges' debut album, a record that a friend had hipped him on to during his time in Gothenburg. It did the trick and also attracted the attention of his roadie neighbour, Mickey 'Rails' Robinson. Over several beers, Nathan learned that Rails had, in fact, once worked as a driver on one of Iggy Pop's tours!

Nat spent much of the first week of school holidays getting ready for Hanna's visit. He'd set up the spare bedroom (complete with an AM radio), a giant teddy bear, a nightlight, and a fluffy, heart-shaped purple cushion. Alana was planning to drop-off some extra blankets and a pillow for Hanna as well. After borrowing a vacuum cleaner from Rails and filling the refrigerator with some tasty food, Nat felt ready to welcome his daughter into his new beachside home.

After phoning first to confirm the details, Nat drove to Amber's on Saturday afternoon to collect Hanna. The exuberance he felt while watching his little girl climb into the car was beyond words, and he looked on proudly as she clicked into her seatbelt, clutching her teddy bear.

'I think strawberry-swirl ice creams are the order of the day!' said Nat, to which Hanna agreed with a squeal. They drove back to Clare, singing loudly to a Beatles cassette while chatting about school.

'I miss you, Daddy,' said Hanna unexpectedly, a comment that filled Nat with both joy and emotion. He smiled back at her.

'Daddy loves you very much, honey,' he replied, smiling all the way back home. After getting acquainted with Checkers, they bought fish and chips from Nugget's before exploring the beach. Later that evening, they sat out on the porch, drinking hot cocoa and searching the sky for shooting stars. It had been a wonderful day. After his daughter had turned in, Baxter sat in silence. He looked up to the heavens and smiled. In that moment, he felt complete contentment.....and he loved it.

Over the course of the next few days, Nat and Hanna made up for the time they'd been apart and shared a lot of laughs. One rainy day, they ventured over to Beldon for a game of ten-pin bowling, followed by a visit to Firebolt, the local amusement arcade. Sometimes, they would walk to Nugget's for a milkshake or just sit on the porch and enjoy reading together. Nathan also taught his daughter how to play solitaire, and she loved it, often taking the deck of cards to bed and playing before falling asleep. Her love of the popular card game had Baxter singing the Neil Sedaka tune of the same name. This, in turn, inspired him to haul out his copy of *The Carpenters Collection* by The Carpenters, who'd tasted success with their take of 'Solitaire' a few years back. Hanna looked on, enthralled, as her Dad nursed his guitar and harmonised with Karen Carpenter's heavenly vocals. Checkers had formed an instant rapport with Hanna and followed her everywhere. The new furry friend had even taken to sleeping on Hanna's bed!

Late one morning, they strolled to the milk bar to get some salt and vinegar chips and a loaf of fresh bread. Baxter had passed on his love of salt and vinegar chip sandwiches to Hanna, and his daughter was now a big fan. As they exited the milk bar, they were stopped by a gaunt, middle-aged lady who asked Nat for some money to buy food. He smiled at her before reaching into his pocket and handing her a couple of dollars.

'Why did you do that, Dad?' asked Hanna as they walked away.

'Because kindness is free,' he replied, smiling.

Alana came over on Friday afternoon, and Nathan was somewhat anxious about this initial meeting between his daughter and new girlfriend. Was it too soon? Some would probably say yes, but he felt comfortable in doing so and went with his heart.

Hanna answered Alana's knock at the door and smiled. Nat could see that Alana was visibly nervous as he introduced them. After a cup of tea and chocolate chip cookies, Alana suggested a walk to the beach to collect shells, and Hanna readily agreed. However, by the time they exited the house, they were greeted by loud thunder and menacing skies. They sat on the porch while the storm passed, with Nat plucking out some acoustic numbers on the guitar to pass the time. He watched as Hanna sang her heart out on a couple of Swedish children's songs, such as 'Lilla Snigel' and 'Katten Och Svansen.'

'I'm going to find a snail now, Daddy!' shrieked Hanna, racing toward the garden bed.

'The first song translates as 'Little Snail' - it's about a child looking for a snail to hug,' explained Nat. '...and believe it or not, if you glance over at Checkers right now trying to chase her tail - that is the very title and meaning of the second song!' They all looked over and laughed at the sight of the black and white cat, as she spun around wildly in pursuit of her tail before darting away.

'She's so funny!' exclaimed Hanna before giving her Dad a cuddle. Alana looked over, basking in the love Nathan felt for his daughter, and smiled.

He is truly someone very special, she thought.

After the clouds had passed, they walked to the beach to gather shells. Baxter held Alana's hand as they watched Hanna run ahead. He felt so alive! Although the light was fading, a rainbow revealed itself, prompting Hanna to run ever faster.

'Come on, Lana, let's find the start of the rainbow!' she shouted. Alana gave Nat a warm look before catching up with Hanna. Although they chased hard, they could not locate where the magical seven colours began their skyward journey. The sight of the two of them running along the shoreline would remain etched in Baxter's heart forever. Cradling handfuls of pretty shells in their tee-shirts, they returned home and cleaned up. The shoreline exercise had given them an appetite - so Alana suggested pizza for dinner, a proposal warmly received by both Nathan and Hanna. Even Checkers seemed excited by the prospect of Alana's visit to Paradise Pizza Parlour to collect dinner, but she had to settle for a tin of pilchards instead!

| 10 |

Term Four

As the winter days ticked away, Baxter continued his residency at the Seahorse Inn. He'd become accustomed to playing Top 40 pap to appease the non-discerning clientele, but would always throw in something obscure by Neil Young or Bob Dylan to keep things interesting. Since his teenage years, sharing his musical tastes with others had always been important to him. Seahorse barflies Pam and Denise seemed to appreciate the deeper cuts he'd play, if their loud applause was any indication.

Nat had settled into his fortnightly routine, driving to collect Hanna, who'd stay until Sunday. Apart from stopping by to say hello, Alana had made an effort not to encroach on their time together, aware that space was vital in allowing her relationship with Hanna to grow. Nat had commenced a 'caffeine-stop' routine on his way back to Clare late on Sundays, making a detour to a small cafe perched at the top of the mountain road. The view of Clare from the escarpment was stunning and he'd often lose track of time, lost in the setting sun. Memories of sipping strong Swedish coffee with Amber a decade earlier would return - of sitting in her car on a cliff top overlooking the North Sea. Aromas have the power to unlock the sweetest of memories.

Gigging again had also rekindled Baxter's passion for songwriting, and over the course of a couple of weeks, he'd penned an up-tempo pop song titled 'Lovesick Sailor,' which he then gave to The Sea Fleas. The song had pretty much written itself after Baxter observed a sailor from a nearby naval base chasing after Charli at the Seahorse. He would usually get hammered on vodka or rum, and after four or five weeks, finally copped the hint that the cute redhead was not interested. Perhaps hearing about Noriko's failed mariner-marriage too often, was enough to make Charli give sailors a wide berth.

Alana had also started sleeping over at Nat's house, and during one late-night conversation over drinks, she con-firmed what he had already suspected: her engagement to Brad had been a violent one. Again, he didn't press her for information, choosing instead to let her talk freely. Turns out Brad was also a control-freak and would explode if things were not done to his standards. He had also kept Alana isolated from her friends and had a cruel streak too, regularly teasing their pets. Baxter felt anger rise inside of him, but it dissipated when he learned that her father, Frank, had once put Brad in the hospital. Never lay a hand on or mistreat the daughter of a tough old combat soldier.

The Sea Fleas continued to make progress as they pre-pared for the school's annual Christmas Concert. The songs they'd settled on were George Harrison's 'My Sweet Lord,' The Beatles' 'Eight Days A Week,' Journey's 'Wheel In The Sky,' and Baxter's recent composition 'Lovesick Sailor.' They also included a take of Blue Öyster Cult's '(Don't Fear) The Reaper' - a light-hearted jab or attempt at humour, given that they would obviously be performing at a religious celebration. Lead vocalist Kristeena, with a wide vocal range, did an admirable job matching Steve Perry's heavenly vocals on the Journey number. For Baxter, though, the star who shone brightest in the band, as he had consistently done in music class, was Rick. Nat looked on in awe as the kid's prowess continued to grow, not only playing by ear but effortlessly composing guitar solos of his own. Now that he had the full support of his parents, the sky really was the limit for young Rick. In case an encore was called for at the concert, he and Baxter had been rehearsing Pink Floyd's 'Wish You Were Here.' The rehearsal experience left Nathan feeling like he was performing with a peer, and not one of his students.

Nat also spent much of his spare time looking over the new releases at Clare's Records and Tapes, which, of course, meant talking music with the store owner. On one occasion, he met an old, long-haired hippie wearing a faded lilac kaftan who grabbed his attention. He observed her as she perused the racks, yet she was aware that Nat was watching her.

'Yeah, I know,' she said, casting him a glare. 'You're gonna ask me where the Demis Roussos LPs are.' - a reference to her vintage clothing. 'Very funny, but I've heard that one before.'

'No, no,' replied Nat. 'You're kaftan looks great. I saw many people wearing them in London back in '69.'

She looked him up and down, and noting his sincerity, lowered her guard.

'I'm Nathan,' he said, extending his hand.
The woman, in her mid-forties, with a peacock feather in her hair, returned his handshake.

'My friends call me Concordia,' she said.

'Demis, by the way, has a massive, powerful voice; and for what it's worth, I own 'Forever and Ever' on 45,' added Nat. 'Great song.'

Concordia's face broke into a broad smile.

'I think he also recorded 'Paperback Writer' early in his career,' chimed Clare, listening in from behind the counter.

'I never doubt the power and knowledge of your Beatle-brain,' offered Nat. Clare smiled back at him, raising her coffee mug in acknowledgement.

Concordia was a potter with a studio five miles out of town, and she turned out to be somewhat of a kindred spirit to Nat. As their friendship grew, he visited her several times, absorbing the peaceful serenity she called home. Her studio was nestled near a lush green rainforest, with no neighbours and an amazing garden that attracted a stunning assortment of wild birds. This, no doubt, inspired a framed poem titled *A Chorus of Bellbirds*, written by Concordia, that hung near the doorway of her studio. When Baxter noticed an acoustic guitar and a collection of Melanie records in the corner of her house, he felt right at home. Concordia was a self-taught musician with limited experience, and felt too shy and self-conscious to perform in front of anyone. Over time, however, Baxter encouraged her to trust in her talent and helped to build up her confidence. For fun, Concordia and Nat would sometimes busk for small change outside Clare's Records. Hanna also took a shine to Concordia, learning from her how to use a potting wheel. As a result, Baxter soon amassed an ever-growing collection of mug and dish creations that could last a lifetime!

One afternoon at school, after the regular parent-teacher meetings had concluded, Carl called Nat into his office. Pip was also present, ready to take some shorthand.

'Uh oh, this looks serious,' said Nat, closing the door behind him.

'Oh, it is, Nathan, but seriously good!' replied Principal Naylor with a smirk.

'The feedback about you we have received from parents is overwhelmingly positive. In fact, many of the students have confided that your music class is the one class they *never* consider skipping!' Pip smiled and nodded in agreement. 'To be honest, I was unsure about taking on a young city teacher with a rock 'n' roll background, but it's been working out great. I want to congratulate you on the positive feedback and say, whatever it is you're doing, please keep on doing it!'

On one unseasonably cold night in December, Baxter sat on his porch with a beer, while Checkers snoozed on his lap, curled under a blanket. A lone mosquito buzzed around the porch light before flying away.

'Cold, clear skies tonight, buddy,' he said. Checkers looked up at him and blinked before resettling herself and returning to sleep. 'And I hope there's clear skies ahead for all of us,' he added, hoping for a happy and trouble-free year ahead. He thought about the past couple of years and reflected on just how miserable and low he had been - and how he had managed to crawl out from that dark and depressing place. Rock 'n' roll, his desire to be happy, and the immense love for his daughter had saved him. His mind then raced back to Gothenburg, to Clapton, and that Blind Faith concert. My gosh, Clapton had gotten him through so many hazy evenings when he was hopelessly lost in the fog - maybe he really was God? He thought of his old friends Edvard and Brigitta, who'd recently had a son named Nils, and the warm image of them as parents made him smile. He missed them. He also missed Sweden and hoped to return for a visit soon. Yawning, he walked inside to get another beer, slipping *After The Gold Rush* on the turntable. *Here's to you, Mr. Young,* he mused, raising his beer at the Hi-Fi. Returning to the porch, he let Checkers inside the house before settling back down. It was past midnight, but time was on his side. No longer would he rush things or fit into someone else's shape.

He shut his eyes and pictured Alana reading Hanna a bedtime story, and the two of them running on the shoreline.

Silence.

It was at that moment, he knew he would be asking for Alana's hand in marriage. The thought was as clear as the sky above. He sat upright and smiled. It felt so right, and deep in his heart, he knew they'd grow old together - the ballerina and the rock 'n' roller. Maybe he had subconsciously penned 'Pristine Heart' for *her* all those years ago.

The Christmas concert coincided with school break-up, an event that was always well attended and a highlight of the school calendar. It was a gathering that also attracted successful alumni, who would return for this event and reflect on their time there. Baxter sensed that one day Rick would make a return visit to the school.

The event was an overwhelming success, with The Sea Fleas answering boisterous calls for an encore. Nathan had, of course, planned for this very situation, and after introducing Rick to the receptive gathering, joined him in a stunning rendition of Pink Floyd's 'Wish You Were Here'. Rick felt a little nervous as he watched his music teacher give his best David Gilmour interpretation. Baxter looked over the receptive crowd and then proudly back at Rick, whose parents were both in tears. Although the concert had run over time, parents, teachers, and fellow students were yelling for more. So, Nat stepped up to the microphone and asked if they wanted to hear one more! He saw Carl sitting in the front row, tapping on his wrist watch - a gesture which indicated it was time to call it a night. Even Pip, who was standing beside him, was calling out for another encore!

'Yeah, why not?!' said Nathan, stumbling back to the mic. 'This *is* a celebration after all, so let's celebrate! Thankyou to everyone for coming along tonight. Music is life, and I encourage you all to consider putting an instrument under the Christmas tree for your kids this year. Now, let's welcome The Sea Fleas back to the stage, who are going to run through 'Junior's Farm' by Paul McCartney and Wings....followed by 'Already Gone' by The Eagles. Let's give 'em a loud round of applause.' Nathan remained on stage, joining in on second guitar and vocal harmonies, and the kids loved it.

Hanna spent much of the rainy Christmas and New Year break in Clare with her Dad. It was one of the happiest times of Baxter's life. On a couple of occasions, Hanna joined other girls at Alana's dance studio, which was fine by Nat as he could pass the time waiting for her at Firebolt. During the break, Hanna even taught her Dad how to bake bread by hand! The image of his seven year old daughter leaning over a bowl, her sleeves rolled up and covered in flour, was forever captured by Nat with his Instamatic camera - a Christmas gift from Alana. On other days, they spent their time making clay figures at Concordia's while listening to Melanie records. Sometimes, they'd stay home and play endless games of quoits, or they would make up funny songs (Santa had brought Hanna a small acoustic guitar for Christmas). Most afternoons, they would walk to the deserted beach, collect dry driftwood and build a fire. Hanna would sit huddled with her Dad for warmth, chatting as the sky turned black. One evening, she fell asleep, and he carried her home.

They welcomed in the new decade with Alana back on the beach, cooking sausages while lighting sparklers and fireworks. Having previously lost so much precious time with her, Baxter cherished the Daddy-daughter memories they were now creating.

| 11 |

A Second Chance

After receiving a couple of requests from students, Nat kicked off the 1980s by offering private guitar lessons. Alana had let him use one of her spare rehearsal rooms, which worked out great since several of his students lived nearby. It also meant he'd get to see more of Alana!

Baxter's neighbour, Mickey Rails, who was working on the national tour for visiting folk singer Cris T. Collins, unexpectedly phoned Nat at school one day. Rails asked if he'd like to open the show for her when it hit Beldon Town Hall, and Baxter couldn't say 'yes' quick enough! The Town Hall housed about 700 people and was a historic venue with much charm. Nat and Alana had attended a violin concerto there, and it was a great-sounding room. The gig with Cris T. Collins in late February was by far the biggest show Baxter had played in years. Yet, he was confident that the weekly gigs at Noriko's bar had him back in peak musical form. Additionally, Baxter's mood was extra buoyant as he was planning to propose to Alana a few days after the gig! Surely, she was going to say 'yes' when he slipped that 0.35-carat diamond ring on her finger! Nat had been saving part of his salary, along with all the proceeds from guitar lessons and gigs, to purchase the engagement ring he had first seen in the front window of R & J Jewelers in Beldon. He was sure Alana was gonna love it!

Cris T. Collins was riding high on the charts with her single 'Falling Apart with a Shattered Heart'. Subsequently, her concert in Beldon on the 29th of February was sold out. Word had spread around Clare High of the music teacher's upcoming support gig, and he was sure that many of his fellow teachers, along with some students, had bought tickets to the show. He would not let himself down, and when the day of the show arrived, Baxter was keen to perform. He'd spent the previous evening alone on the porch with Checkers, going through his repertoire.

Before the show, Nathan had a pre-gig drink with Alana at a local wine bar to help quell any nerves. A short while later, she planted a good-luck kiss on his cheek and then watched him enter the backstage area. He closed his eyes for a moment and envisioned himself as a teenager, before confidently stepping onto the stage at 7:30PM.

The brightness of the spotlight made him glad he was wearing dark shades - a trick he'd learned from Edvard. Baxter adjusted the microphone, greeted the crowd, and began his thirty-minute set with a cover of Lynyrd Skynyrd's 'Simple Man'. His voice was clear and loud as it echoed around the venue. He strained and strummed, and the audience moved their heads in time with him. Next up was 'Angel' by Hendrix, performed in the style of Rod Stewart circa '72. A sublime take of the Joan Baez hit 'Diamonds and Rust' held the crowd's attention, as did a stark interpretation of Lennon's 'Working Class Hero'. The crowd were now his. A resurrected and revamped version of his own composition, 'Pristine Heart,' got a loud response - even Chris T. stood side-stage to see what all the commotion was about. He closed out the set with a raspy cover of Kiss' 'Hard Luck Woman,' which ended a triumphant performance. Baxter bowed and waved, high-fiving Rails as he left the stage. 'You woulda been proud, Ed. You woulda been proud, brother,' he mused.

The day after the gig, Baxter headed to Port Stafford to pick up a few groceries. He could also kill some time playing the pinnies at Tilt! Afterwards, he sat in a cafe, contemplating how to ask for Alana's hand in marriage. He'd decided on a little ruse, inviting her for a midweek dinner instead of their usual Friday/Saturday routine, hoping she wouldn't suspect anything. He also mentioned that he wanted to discuss the possibility of her teaching yoga lessons at Clare High - which was, in fact, true. It was an initiative of Carl's that he'd been asking Baxter about. With the proposal taking shape, he stopped by the Surfrider restaurant before leaving Port Stafford and made a reservation for the upcoming Wednesday.

'Trust in your feelings, Baxter. You've found your soulmate,' he said aloud, while walking to his car.

The 5th of March was a Wednesday, and held no significance to most - except Nathan. It was the day he would ask Alana to be his wife, and he recognized it as a truly momentous occasion. A decade ago, he'd happily tied the knot with Amber, believing that the relationship would last forever - and for a long, long time, he thought it would. He sat on the edge of his bed and looked down at the velvet ring box which housed the engagement ring. Checkers rubbed against his legs. *You deserve to be happy, Baxter, and true love has entered your life. She is your star.* He silently nodded, snapped the box shut, fed Checkers, then made his way to school.

Nervous excitement raced through his veins across the school day, and Nat found it hard to focus. Several teachers were still back-slapping him about the previous Friday's concert with Cris T. Collins, which he found humbling. A couple of them even expressed their desire to take up guitar lessons with Nat, so that was a positive result! After signing off, Nat changed into a suit and tie, earning a wolf whistle from Pip!

'What's with the nice clothes? she asked. 'A special dinner maybe?'

Yet Nat remained silent, smiled politely, then made his way to Beldon to pick up Alana. He changed cassettes as he drove, but eventually settled on the local station. As he pulled up to the Perry residence, Queen's recent single 'Crazy Little Thing Called Love' blared fatefully from the speakers. The irony was not lost on him as he looked down at the illuminated radio dial. Nat removed the key from the ignition, exited the vehicle and strode to the front door.

Alana was surprised to see Baxter dressed so smartly.

'What's the occasion?' she asked.

'Oh, this?' he replied, looking over his attire. 'I was in a fancy mood. I fancied being fancy.'

'Well, you look very handsome, Nat.' He bowed his

head and gestured towards the car.

'Thankyou for changing your schedule,' he said, opening the passenger door for her.

When they arrived at the Surfrider, Alana noticed an acoustic guitar and a mic stand set up in the corner, but thought nothing of it. After a delicious seafood meal, accompanied by a locally produced white wine, Nathan, Alana and the other diners were interrupted by the maître d', who garnered everyone's attention by ringing a small dinner bell.

'Ladies and gentlemen,' he said, 'I apologise for interrupting your meal. However, we have a special guest in the restaurant this evening - a local musician with an important message. Please give a warm welcome to the stage for Mr. Nathan Baxter.'

'What's going on?' asked Alana, with raised eyebrows.

Nat gave her a knowing smile, removed the napkin from his lap, stood up, and excused himself before making his way to the small makeshift stage.

'Hello everyone. My name is Nathan Baxter. Thank you for allowing me to briefly interrupt your dinner. This is a very special evening for myself and my beautiful girlfriend over there, Alana. To commemorate this occasion, I'll be performing a special song - written in 1964 but truly timeless. It captures everything I want to say to her.' He adjusted the guitar strap over his shoulder and took a calming breath.

The other diners, as well as the staff, sat watching as Nat delivered an exquisite rendition of The Beatles' song 'And I Love Her.' His vocals were clean and concise - and the on-lookers showed their appreciation for the unannounced performance, by giving him a loud round of applause at the completion of the song.

Nat rejoined Alana at the table and noticed her blushing. Before she could speak, he moved his chair closer, pulled the ring box from his pocket and opened it.

'You've changed my world, Alana Perry, and I want to spend the rest of my life with you - as your husband. Will you grow old with me?'

Alana gasped, covering her mouth with her hands. She stood up and burst into tears.

'Yes of course!' she squealed, squeezing him tight. By now, the other dinner guests had figured out what was going on, prompting a second, even louder round of applause. Nat held Alana in his arms, savouring the moment. Over coffee and after-dinner mints, a beaming Alana could not take her eyes off the engagement ring. She repeatedly held it at arm's length, admiring its beauty.

'Surprised?' Nat asked.

'Very much so, and also very happy,' she replied, leaning over to kiss him.

They set the wedding date for the 8th of August. Although Alana was keen to be a September bride, Nat was reluctant due to the omen associated with remarrying precisely ten years after his first marriage to Amber. Even though the situation was entirely different from his first marriage in September 1970, he was not going to take any chances. True, a (cute) black cat crossed his path at home every day, and although Nathan was not superstitious, he still wanted his future marriage to begin with a positive outlook. It just felt 'off' to get remarried exactly a decade later, so if that meant shifting the big day to one month earlier, then so be it.

It was five months to the wedding day, but Alana was already anxious about the ceremony. Nat, on the other hand, was fine with the low-key event they had discussed and assured her everything would be OK. Now that he was a little older and wiser, Nat believed that it was less about the expensive, lavish ceremony and more about the couple and the love that they shared. For Baxter, it was all about one thing: true love and simple happiness. With this in mind, he'd suggested a small beachside gathering with only a few close friends and family. Hanna would be a flower girl. Alana, who'd fallen head over heels for Nat, was happy to wed him anywhere and anytime. Convinced that she too had found her soulmate, she agreed that a small beachside wedding sounded beautiful.

Baxter continued his regular slot at the Seahorse Inn. However, after his one-off 'proposal' gig at the Surfrider, the owner offered him a monthly slot there, which he happily accepted. Live bookings were scarce on the coast so he was grateful for the opportunity. He had also settled into a somewhat regular routine with Hanna, although her mother remained 'unnecessarily difficult' - that's how he described it. She continued to show him no courtesy or respect, and he often wondered if she ever would. At night, Nat would sometimes sit on the porch with Checkers, letting his mind wander. He could never understand how someone with whom he once shared so much could come to detest him so greatly. He knew that deep down, a part of him was damaged by her incessant bitterness. He tried and gave so much of himself during his marriage to Amber, until he could give no more. Yet, even now, he hoped that his ex-wife would one day find happiness.

After his proposal to Alana, Nat had also been spending more time with her parents, Frank and Margaret. Her mother was quite an accomplished ukulele player, and on one occasion, brought out a handcrafted uke that she'd purchased in Hawaii some years back. The sound that emanated from the instrument was superb, and when she dueted with Nat on his acoustic guitar, the mood in the Perry's living room became bright and comfortable. They were warming to him.

As the weeks ticked by, Baxter found himself busier than ever at school, which also included evening and weekend work. He wasn't too keen on the extra hours, but they were short a couple of teachers and that meant covering shifts. Besides, Nat didn't want to let Carl down, so he rearranged his schedule to suit. He was, however, adamant that work would not impact his time with Hanna. But he hadn't seen Alana as often as he would've liked, and it wasn't due to their schedules; she simply hadn't stopped by as much.

Actually, he first noticed something when he made her a cup of tea in bed one morning. Alana was unusually quiet, and when he quizzed her, she told him she felt tired. Truth be told, she *had* been putting in a lot of late nights at the dance studio, so Nat brushed it off. However, when she cancelled on a planned picnic with little Hanna, he sensed that there was more to this than just being overworked. So, one Sunday evening in late May, Nat decided to drive straight to the Perry house after returning Hanna to her Mum's.

'Sorry Nathan, you've just missed her,' said Frank. 'She's taken Button out for a walk.'

Baxter smiled and accepted Frank's offer of a coffee while he waited for Alana to return. When she arrived home thirty or so minutes later, she seemed surprised to see him there.

'I thought that was your car parked outside,' she said, removing the leash from the small terrier.'

'Well, the big day in August is fast approaching, and I know you've been busy at the studio. So, I thought I'd swing by on my way home to talk over a couple of ideas I've had,' explained Nat.

'I'm glad you did,' she replied softly, 'because that's what I've been wanting to talk to you about.'

Her father was perceptive enough to know that his daughter needed to talk in private, so he excused himself to join Margaret in the kitchen. Alana sat on the edge of the sofa nursing Button. She leaned her head to one side while gently scratching the dog's head. Button closed her eyes, enjoying the affection.

Silence.

Alana looked out of the window before speaking softly.

'I don't think I can marry you, Nathan.'

In an instant, he felt his heart sink.

'But why?' he asked. 'What's this all about, Alana?'

She pursed her lip and sat silently.

He noticed tears welling in her eyes, so handed her some tissues.

'I still carry emotional scars from being with Brad, who I truly believed was *the one.* The pain and hurt which he caused me runs deeper than I initially thought. I'm just not sure if I'm ready.'

Baxter sat deep in thought, considering this.

'Are you frightened of being hurt?' he asked.

'You're not a violent man,' she replied, then realised he was alluding to her previous broken heart. 'No, I mean, maybe, ahm, yeah I am a little,' she added. 'And marriage is a big commitment.'

He sat silent for a minute, then stood up and walked over to embrace her.

'Yes, marriage is a big commitment. But if it's built on friendship and respect, and if the hearts are pure and the love is true, it's easy. I am not Brad. Trust in your feelings. I love you, Alana,' he said in a low voice before kissing her softly and exiting the house.

Although it was getting late, a despondent Nat stopped off at the Seahorse Inn for a couple of drinks before Noriko closed up. Sure, he was aware that booze could not mend a wounded heart, but he just didn't feel like going home - and although the former 'Mama-san' was a great listener, Baxter did not share his sad news with Noriko. He instead sat absorbed, as she regaled him with the story of the time she saw the Japanese band Off Course perform in Yokohama back in '72.

'I have a concert review of it somewhere. Actually, you're a big music fan aren't you Nathan-san?'

He raised his glass at her and nodded.

'My sister just sent me the latest Off Course single, and it's amazing. I'll put it in the jukebox next week for you to hear. Sugoi ne!'

'That'd be cool,' he replied.

'Let me find that review….' she said.

He watched as Noriko danced away, humming the melody to the Off Course song 'Sayonara'. She then disappeared under the bar and began sifting through some old copies of *Music Life Magazine*.

'Maybe some other time,' said Nat. 'Tonight's a school night.'

Noriko gave him a bag of spring rolls along with a six-pack of Ashton Ale, which she told him he could work off. Baxter was starving and hungrily tore into one of the rolls before reaching his car. He winced as the filling was hot and burnt the roof of his mouth. Hungry, he pressed on, chugging down one of the beers to soothe his pain. Baxter placed the bottle on the roof of his car, pulled the keys from his pocket, and arched his head back to admire the stars and the half-moon above. The sky was clear and beautiful that night, yet it carried a tinge of sadness. With a heavy heart, he let out a sigh.

'Bring her back to me,' he said aloud, 'She's my angel.'

The following day at school, Baxter felt like he was in a fog. Pip sensed something was up and cornered him in the staff room during lunch. She assured Nat that Alana would soon come to her senses, noting that he was 'something pretty special.' Pip was blushing but sincere, and her heart-felt sentiments lifted his spirits.

'Thanks, Pip,' Nat said.

'You bet,' she replied.

When he got home, he fed Checkers, and then headed over to Nugget's for some food. He ordered a hamburger with the lot and a chocolate milkshake, although it wasn't a traditional shake; rather, it was flavoured milk consumed from a pint bottle. Local kids would grab a bottle from the fridge, peel back the foil cover, take a gulp, and then ask Nugget to squirt in their favourite flavour. It was something which Nugget's had become famous for, at least among the kids at Clare High. And there was no bigger kid than Baxter, who glugged on his chocolate-flavoured milk while selecting a song on the jukebox.

'Give me ten minutes, Nat. I gotta cut some onions,' shouted Nugget over the music.

'Throw in some hot chips and potato scallops too, will ya?' replied Baxter. As he reached into his pocket for change, Nat sang along loudly to Hendrix's 'Hey Joe' while taking another swig from the bottle. 'Nugget, don't you ever remove Jimi from your jukebox, OK?' Nat said. The cook couldn't hear over the music, along with the sizzle from the hot plate. Nathan's gaze then focused on a new pinball machine in the takeaway store, honouring the rock band Kiss. 'Outta sight!' he exclaimed, rolling in a coin. Half an hour later, Nathan lost his final ball but was happy to have nabbed the high score. He doused one of the scallops in vinegar, shoved it in his mouth, then exited the store with the food.

Once home, he ate his greasy dinner on the porch with Checkers, who happily consumed the chips Nat had dropped. After finishing his meal, he scrunched the food wrapper into a ball and wiped his hands on his jeans. He picked up his guitar, propped his feet on the verandah, and played a slow, sorrowful take of James Taylor's 'Fire and Rain'. Cracking open another beer, Baxter then carried the guitar inside the house before awakening the Hi-Fi. On the turntable rested *461 Ocean Boulevard,* the Clapton album that flowed through his life like an audio stream. He lowered the stylus and stood motionless, trancelike in front of the speakers. It was track two that did it, though; 'Give Me Strength.' Baxter downed the last of the ale and closed his eyes, absorbing Clapton's lyrics. He was gonna need every bit of strength to get through this. As the music played, he looked over the album jacket. He flipped it over and focused on the photograph of Clapton sitting on a chair at Florida's Golden Beach, strumming an acoustic guitar. Why was there such a deep connection with this record? It was an album that seemed to speak to him, a record with which he identified - and this was something Baxter took great comfort in. At around 1:30AM, he opened the last of the beers and then fell asleep on the sofa.

Baxter was awakened by the constant drone of a car engine. For twenty minutes, the owner depressed the accelerator and revved the engine. On and on it went, drowning out the shoreline sounds Nathan had become accustomed to.

'Christ, it's warm already,' he murmured, referring to the nearby vehicle's V8 engine. He rolled over and glanced at the clock. 'Gah! I'm gonna be late,' he groaned. Checkers sat watching her owner as he scurried to the shower. She arched her back and then made herself comfortable on his warm woollen blanket. Remarkably, Baxter arrived at school just as the second bell rang out. Unshaven and bleary-eyed, he managed to grab a cup of coffee and dart into the music room right on schedule.

'Hey, Mr. B, look what song I figured out!' yelled one of the students from the back of the room. It was Stevie 'Strings' McMillan, who had plugged his Fender Strat into one of the large practice amps and was playing the lick to 'Layla' rather loudly. The lanky kid with a long ponytail earned the nickname 'Strings' due to his obsession with the guitar. While he didn't have the natural flair of his fellow classmate Rick, Nathan nevertheless admired the passion he possessed.

'That's damn cool, Stevie. And as much as I love Derek and The Dominos, I'm fairly certain, as I've mentioned before, that Miss McDonnell and her mathematics class next door do not - especially at this early hour.' 'Strings' switched off the amp and sat down just as Miss McDonnell's head peered into the room. Nathan acknowledged her and pretended to pray for forgiveness. The older teacher scowled and returned to her class. 'May I add, though, brother Stevie, that lick was note-perfect and would no doubt get the nod of approval from both Clapton and, of course, Duane Allman from the Allman Brothers, who I believe came up with that iconic guitar part.' The students nodded and Baxter grinned. He had the best job in the world.

Over the next couple of weeks, Baxter immersed himself in work to help take his mind off Alana. It didn't work, as everywhere he went, there was something to remind him of her - not least of which were her pretty clothes hanging in his wardrobe. Although she'd had cold feet about the marriage, Nat was happy to give her time and space to work through her feelings. He adored her, and they were deeply in love; that was not going to change. He was, of course, very disappointed, yet he was just happy to have Alana in his life.

Nat turned the big three-zero on the 18th of June and wanted no fuss. Not that anyone in Clare knew it was his birthday. At least, that's what he thought. However, when he arrived at school, the balloons and streamers in the staff room indicated that his secret was out. He looked suspiciously at Pip as she tried hard to contain her smile.

'Yep, it was me,' she confessed, 'And also Carl. You once let slip that you shared your birthday with Paul Mc-Cartney, and I guess he remembered.' Nat had hands thrust at him to be shaken - some from other teachers he barely knew. But he was happy for the attention and doubly delighted by the box of iced donuts he spied on the table. That was breakfast. He'd hoped that Alana would've swung by to help him celebrate, but he was buoyed just the same to find a card she had dropped off in his letterbox. Best of all, though, was a birthday call from Hanna, who'd phoned the school office just before he exited. Her giggles and the pure excitement in her voice made his spirit soar, and it was moments like this that defined true happiness.

One wet and rainy weekend, Baxter cancelled his food shopping expedition to Port Stafford, preferring to stay indoors. He spent the evenings writing songs and most of the daylight hours asleep. Late on Sunday, a light mist had blanketed the seaside town, so Nat headed over to the beach to escape the gloom. He brought with him a book, two beers, and some coins for the telephone to call Alana. With the grey skies and cold temperature, Baxter had the beach all to him-self. He managed to locate some dry driftwood and then lit a small fire. There was something comforting about sitting in front of the flames. Baxter watched as they danced back and forth, illuminating his face and the pages of the book. He warmed his hands and then stood up to observe the ocean. Far out in the dark sea, two bobbing green lights from a distant fishing trawler gazed back at him. He sat back down and resumed reading, building up the fire when necessary.

'I thought I'd find you here,' said a familiar voice. He looked up to see Alana walking towards him, her long flowing hair being caressed by the breeze. She was wearing a dark blue windcheater over a cream sweater, and even in the fading light, looked gorgeous.

'I find solace here,' replied Nat. 'You know that.'

'I know you do,' she whispered. 'It's one of the reasons why I love you so much.'
Nathan looked up at her and smiled.

'It's also a great place to think…and write…and read,' he added, holding up the book. They stared at each other for the longest time - soundtracked by the sound of the surf. No words were needed. Sometimes, when a couple are deep in love, everything is said in the silence. She sat down next to him on the sand, keeping her hands in her pockets for warmth.

'Well, I've been doing some thinking myself.'
Nathan listened while staring at the smoke wafting from a piece of damp driftwood.

'What are you doing on the 8th of August?' she asked, her face breaking into a smile. Elated, Nat grabbed her and squeezed her tightly.

'Really? Are you serious?' he asked. Alana was crying tears of joy and he pulled her close to him. 'I'm speechless! This is so wonderful. I just love you so much.'

'I am happy when I am with you,' she whispered quietly.

They remained wrapped in each other's arms until the fire died out.

That night, Nathan was so happy that he couldn't sleep. He got up, made a cup of tea, and drank it in bed while listening to his transistor radio. Checkers jumped up, and he gently stroked the back of her head. She responded to the affection by purring loudly. He shut his eyes and smiled, overjoyed by the realisation that the wedding was back on. After some time, Baxter yawned wearily and finally fell back to sleep, oblivious to the airwave rants of early morning insomniacs phoning in to the local talkback radio station. A smile graced his face as he snored softly.

With the wedding going ahead, the next few days were spent rescheduling things such as invitations, flowers, catering, and organising a pre-wedding gathering at the Southern Anchor for friends and colleagues. The ceremony itself was to be an intimate beach gathering for family and close friends. When Nat told Hanna that she was going to be a flower girl, she was elated.

'Do I get to dress up like a princess?' she asked. 'Can we buy a dress that sparkles and glitters?'

'Absolutely,' her Dad replied. 'And you are going to look very, very pretty. Maybe even prettier than the bride.' Hanna giggled with delight.

Nathan continued to gig and earn some extra cash from private lessons. He planned on performing a song he'd written for Alana on their wedding day and was very happy with how the tune was progressing. He'd also been making some adjustments to his house to ensure that Alana felt more comfortable when she moved in permanently. He'd learned that dancers owned a lot of clothes - at least this one did. Although many of her clothes were already hanging in his wardrobe, he brought in another cupboard to give her more space. Despite soon being remarried, Nat loved his current abode and was in no hurry to rush out and buy a property elsewhere. This tranquil place was now a part of him, and his journey of rediscovery also centred around the ocean and the laid-back lifestyle. He was determined not to repeat the mistakes he had made with Amber. Nathan Baxter was well and truly back. Never again would he fit into someone else's shape and allow himself to be so dominated. With Alana, he felt comfortable. He didn't have to act a certain way; he could just be 'Nat'. He was 'home' and he was now ready to write a new chapter in his life.

On the Friday night before the wedding, many of Nat's colleagues gathered at The Southern Anchor to celebrate his upcoming marriage. Even Kimberly and Terry from South Fletcher High were in attendance, along with Concordia and his neighbour Mickey-Rails, who looked every inch the roadie in his sleeveless Wings 1975 tour shirt.

'You just need a flashlight in your back pocket, a roll of gaffer tape in your hand, and you're ready to rock,' laughed Nat. Rails smiled.

A couple of parents from school, with whom Nathan had developed a strong rapport, also came along. It was a memorable evening too, with both Carl and even Pip making speeches which Nathan found very humbling. After dinner, most of the guests finished up at The Seahorse, where a drunken Nat was pretty much forced onto the stage to perform an impromptu set. Charli the barmaid provided backup vocals on a couple of songs, including The Beatles' 'In My Life.' Despite not knowing all the lyrics, she held her own and appeared comfortable in that role.

'Sounding really great there, Charli,' slurred Baxter at song's end. 'Hey, have you ever considered getting outta Clare? See some of the world maybe?' She leaned in close to him.

'Actually, Nathan,' she replied, hinting at a change while out of earshot of Noriko. 'The big city lights are calling me.' She tapped her nose, gave him a knowing wink, stepped off the stage, and returned to her duties.

'Good for you,' he answered loudly, nodding in approval. For old time's sake, Baxter dragged Rails up on stage; himself no slouch on the guitar, for a rowdy run through of Clapton's 'Cocaine', followed by a stripped back version of 'White Room'. Before the evening was over, Nat's curiosity got the better of him, and he asked Mickey how he got his nickname.

His neighbour looked at him over his dai-jockey glass and grinned.

'Many people assume it's cos I'm outta control - like I'm 'off the rails', but in fact, it comes from a long tour I once did with that rock band, Sinners Mist.'

'Oh, I remember them!' exclaimed Nat. 'From Wales, sounded a lot like Black Sabbath, right?'

'Yeah, that's them. Actually, the spooky and dark image they portrayed was quite laughable, and those guys were, in fact, pretty tame. On the off nights, the band and crew would go ten pin-bowling, something I really stink at - I mean, I think during one ten-frame game I scored a total of 12 points. Anyway, the bass player - I forget his name - started calling me 'Rails', as in 'guard rails' - y'know, that device they use to stop you from rolling a gutter ball. It's usually used at kids' birthday parties.' He drank the remainder of his beer and rested the glass down on a coaster before continuing. 'I think on the final night of that tour, his tech handed him his bass guitar before they hit the stage, and the fretboard *may have* been caked in superglue. Although I wouldn't know anything about that,' he said with a smirk, then walked to the bar for a refill. Nat shook his head chuckling.

Although the weather in August was unseasonably cold, Baxter awoke to a refreshing blue sky on the morning of the 8th. Hanna eagerly entered his room with a cup of tea as he sat up, listening to the radio.

'Dad, Checkers slept on my bed last night. She is getting so heavy!'

'I know. I think old Bert, the fisherman from down the street, feeds her his off-cuts when he comes home from the wharf. She's morphing into a black-and-white toad fish,' replied Nat. Hanna burst out laughing, spilling tea onto the bed. The laughter stopped as she glanced nervously at her Dad, half expecting a scolding.

'Hey, don't worry about it,' he replied. 'It's just tea, and it's time I washed this stinky ol' blanket anyway.' His reassuring smile made her smile, and they chuckled all the way into the kitchen. He never believed in scolding kids when they made a mistake like that; accidents happen. Move on.

As they made another cup of tea, he told her the story of an incident from when *he* was a boy, which involved a frozen soda bottle.

'When I removed it from the freezer and opened it, the bottle exploded like a cola rocket fountain.....all over the kitchen ceiling!' laughed Nat. Hanna broke into another fit of laughter, only this time the giggles led to hiccups. 'It was a waste of good cola,' he added with a wink.

Later that afternoon, Nat's parents arrived and he was happy to see them. They hadn't seen much of their granddaughter in recent months, so they made up for lost time by spoiling her with hugs and kisses, as well as some *Pink Princess* popping candy which they'd purchased on their long drive to Clare. Nat watched as his daughter took her grandparents' hands and proudly showed them her bedroom. He felt a warmth rise inside his chest as he watched on. Nat knew that these precious, fleeting moments in time are the ones to really cherish - the only ones that matter. Like Hanna, he hadn't seen his parents in some time, and it was evident that they had aged a lot. His recently retired Dad looked weary, and he had been in poor health lately. He sat with Hanna on her bed and read her a story from a book she'd handed him. Nathan's father, sensing that his son was watching, looked up and smiled. It was the smile of a contented man, overjoyed to be spending time with his only grandchild - a child who they'd once called 'the light of their life'. Nat's parents were also casualties of his divorce, and it was something that would often weigh heavily on him.

Hanna managed to persuade her grandparents to take

her to the ice cream shop during their brief visit as well, but only on the proviso that they try 'Strawberry-swirl!'

'Can we go to Beldon for ice cream today, pleaaaase?' begged Hanna. The three adults looked lovingly at her and smiled.

'We can't go today, sweetie. Your Daddy is getting married,' explained Hanna's grandmother. Nathan rested his hand on his Mum's shoulder and kissed her on the top of her head.

'Indeed he is,' he replied, 'And we'd better get moving. But first, let's make some coffee.' Whilst Hanna read books in her room, the three adults all sat around the kitchen table, waiting for the drip coffee machine to do its thing. Nathan's mother fidgeted with a teaspoon before speaking.

'It's such a shame, Nat, that things couldn't be better with Amber, if only for Hanna's sake.' He pursed his lips, paused, and then smiled at the warmth in his mother's words.

'Y'know, Mum, I've really tried, and even after everything, I carry no resentment and hope she finds happiness. We had some wonderful times, and I have many memories, but now I try to only recall the happy ones. But I agree, it doesn't, and never had to be like this,' finished Nat. He poured the coffee and watched as his mother, deep in thought, stirred milk into her black coffee. 'Don't worry, Mum. Hanna will find her way, and I will always be the best Dad I can be.'

Nathan and Alana had decided on a late afternoon ceremony, hoping to take advantage of the sun setting over the ocean. As fate would have it, the bride and groom were blessed on their special day with a pinkish-blue coloured sky, which created a peaceful, romantic ambiance. Baxter strode proudly from his car toward the sheltered beach area where the ceremony would take place. He held Hanna's hand while the other clutched his acoustic guitar. Nat greeted some of the small gathering who were sipping white wine and chatting happily. After twenty or so minutes, he glanced to his left as a car door slammed. The vision he witnessed would remain with him forever; Alana was wearing a white, pleated chiffon dress. She looked stunning. Her hair was pinned back by two elegant floral clips, and hidden behind the thin lace veil that covered her face was a nervous smile. She was flanked by her father, Frank, who held her arm as they walked together. Nathan stood, mesmerised by her beauty until she was standing beside him.

'You look like a goddess….the goddess of dance,' he whispered. Alana was beaming. A local celebrant named Lorraine oversaw proceedings and spoke to the assembled guests about the meaning of marriage. Nat smiled down at Hanna as she handed the wedding rings from a small cushion, first to Alana, and then to him. Nathan and Alana exchanged vows and carefully slid the bands onto each other's fingers. They shared a secretive look, as only they knew that their respective rings were engraved with each other's names inside. After they exchanged vows, two white doves were released and soared high into the sky. Nathan pulled Alana close to him and kissed her softly. They embraced, and the small gathering applauded their approval, with the loudest responses coming from Pip and Nathan's Mum. Baxter glanced over at Frank who nodded enthusiastically. Dads and daughters - it's a special bond that only a father can understand. Baxter returned the nod as if to say, 'She's in good hands.' After a toast, Nathan swung the acoustic guitar over his shoulder and sang his recent composition to Alana. It was heartfelt and sincere, containing the lyrics: '*And I will love her forever, through any kind of weather. She is the light in my life, my beautiful wife - Alana.*'

Tears of happiness rolled down both the new bride's face and that of Nathan's mother. Affirming his love for Alana through song in front of friends and family meant more to him than any speech ever could. At the conclusion of the song, Nat continued playing, delivering a powerful performance of the John Lennon song 'Love'. He smiled over at Pip, who was dabbing her moist eyes with a tissue. Lorraine, the marriage celebrant, broke the silence with another buoyant handclap, prompting the others to join in, congratulating the newly wedded couple with hugs and kisses. Some of the guests showered the couple with confetti.

After the wedding, all the guests assembled at Nat's place to celebrate. The alcohol flowed freely, and the Hi-Fi worked overtime, cranking out a selection of mid-to-late '60s music. At one stage, all the guests joined in unison, singing loudly to the track 'Heart of Stone' by the Rolling Stones. Nat looked over at his Mum, singing her heart out, surprised that she knew the lyrics to the song.

'How could your father and I *not* have learned these songs? You played them loudly, over and over and over again when you were a teenager!' Nat smiled back at her with pride. They never once questioned his passion for music when he was a kid and were always supportive, even buying him guitar strings and tablature books. His Dad had also contributed most of the funds for Nat's first amp, and their presence today meant a lot to him. Like any parent, they were just pleased to see their child happy. A voice interrupted Nat's thoughts...

'Hey Baxter, how about some Blind Faith?' shouted Rails, flicking through Nathan's LP collection.

'I've gotta much better idea, brother,' said Nat, lifting his guitar from its stand.

Cradling a tall glass of wine, Alana nestled herself next to her new husband on the sofa. The wedding guests looked on affectionately, as the couple performed a note-perfect version of Blind Faith's 'Can't Find My Way Home,' followed by Neil Young's 'Cinnamon Girl.' Although Nat's vocal range was within reach of Steve Winwood's, having Alana help out on the higher parts worked well and added a beautiful touch to their day. If she was shy, she didn't show it, and Nathan was beaming. Carl, who'd been downing several Ashton Ales, stood up and drunkenly read out some telegrams. He also told the gathering about how Nathan had brought so much positivity to the school and that employing him was one of his best-ever decisions as the school principal. Uneasy on his feet, Pip assisted him onto a chair and later helped him into a taxi.

When the clock struck 10:00PM, Hanna was exhausted and sound asleep. By a quarter past two, the party had wound down and the house was quiet. Alana was asleep, as were Nat's Mum and Dad, who had bunked down on a sofa bed in the lounge room. Nat sat out on the porch, nursing one final bottle of Ashton Ale with his feet up, gazing at the moon. Checkers lay asleep on his lap.

| 12 |

Friendship and Daffodils

Nat awoke early one Saturday morning in August of 1990, as he had a busy day ahead. He let Alana sleep in, then roused Hanna from her slumber with a hot cup of tea.

'Hey honey, we'd better get moving.' he said. Hanna sat up and yawned, nodded, then took a sip of tea. Nat followed the sound of hungry meows emanating from the kitchen and poured Checkers some warm milk. He looked at her lovingly, softly petting the side of her face as she lapped up the milk. Checkers was now thirteen years old, and although not as agile, remained a much-loved member of the Baxter clan. She'd also had to adjust to sharing living space with not one, but two dogs: Alana's little dog Button and Snuffles, a small Maltese Terrier belonging to Hanna. When Snuffles was a puppy, she had an allergy that caused her to have sneezing fits, hence her name. The two dogs were sound asleep, so Nat snuck past and let them be. *Let sleeping dogs lie,* he mused, then laughed aloud when he realised that those two hounds were scared of their own shadows.

After making coffee, Baxter stopped by the local florist to purchase two bunches of flowers: orchids and a large bunch of daffodils. This bright yellow flower commemorates the tenth year of marriage, and he wanted to surprise Alana with a big bouquet when he returned from the airport. The orchids were for his Dad, or rather, for his Dad's grave, to be precise. Nat visited him regularly at his final resting place, Beldon Cemetery, which overlooked the ocean. Losing him to heart disease a few months after his marriage to Alana was tough. Even as a boy, Nathan sensed how harmful cigarettes were and the damage that they were inflicting to his 'pack-a-day' Dad. Concerned, he'd even started hiding his father's ciggies, but in the end, it was futile. By visiting his Dad and chatting, Nat had found a way to help heal the pain - this was his initial way of coping with the grief he'd felt and it became a routine he continued. The sadness never fully subsided, even after all this time. But Nat was determined to keep his memory alive and would often talk and play 'remember when' with his Dad, as if he were sitting alongside him. He placed his outstretched hand on the bronze plaque and touched it lightly, farewelling his Dad until next time. Nat and Hanna walked back to the car, and once they had settled in, he started the engine. She'd just graduated from Clare High and was chatting excitedly about the upcoming School Formal - a glitzy affair where the boys rented tuxedos and the girls spent up big on ball gowns.

'Are you *sure* you don't want Dad and his old pal Edvard to perform next week? The return of Håkansson and

Baxter - first gig in twenty years!' exclaimed Nat.

'If it was up to me, Dad, you know I'd say yes,' she replied. He looked over at his daughter in the front seat and smiled. Being a dad was his greatest achievement in life. She held the bunch of daffodils at an angle to prevent the water at the base from spilling. 'They're pretty,' said Hanna, leaning in to smell the petals. 'Dad, it's John Lennon!' she exclaimed, noting the song that had come on the car radio. Baxter nodded, gazing ahead at the road, chasing down a memory. He thought back to that memorable August day on the beach. How pretty Alana had looked. How some guests had cried when he expressed his love for her through a John Lennon song. His face then darkened as he recalled that he, along with millions of others, would be shedding tears of sadness four months later following Lennon's senseless murder in New York City. It was a day that Baxter would never forget. He cleared his throat and quickly switched the radio off.

'Hey, why don't we put on the new Clapton album, *Journeyman*? I picked it up yesterday at Clare's CD and Video Vault.'

'But Dad, you don't have a CD player. When are we gonna get one?' moaned Hanna.

'It's also released on audio cassette,' he grinned. 'I had Clare order me in a copy.'

Hanna sighed and reached for the cassette case stowed behind the driver's seat.

They were on their way to the international airport to pick up his old friends, Edvard and Brigitta, who were flying in from Sweden. With them was their son, Erik, who was two years younger than Hanna and, according to his Dad, 'a fine young bass player!' Nat and Alana had travelled to Europe six years earlier, and after staying with the Håkansson's, wanted to return the favour. Ed and Brigitta had moved from Gothenburg to Linköping some time ago to care for Brigitta's elderly mother. Music had now become a hobby for Ed. He had swapped his bass guitar for ovens and rolling pins some time ago, and now he and Brigitta ran one of the busiest bakeries in the city.

For several minutes, Baxter tapped his fingers on the steering wheel in time with the music, nodding his approval.

'Do you think Ed and Brigitta can bake us some limpa bread when they're here?' asked Hanna, ejecting the tape.

'Oh you bet!' answered Nat. 'I have a craving for some Swedish fika pastries right now. And for your Dad, it's not just a morning tea treat; I can eat them any time!' Hanna laughed and turned up the volume on a song she liked.

"First week in at number three, that's Rick Raven with the brand new single Starlight,' said the on-air DJ. 'The reviews I've read so far are positive, and if this forthcoming album is anything like its triple-platinum-selling predecessor, then rock fans are in for a real treat. The new album, titled 'Medusa,' has a release date of September the 2nd, with the first thousand copies pressed on coloured vinyl. How cool is that? Rick Raven, as you all know hails from the seaside town of Clare. After slaying 'em in America, he is embarking on a national tour in December, including a hometown show at the Lincoln Pavillion on the 15th, proudly presented by

FM 114.9. All next week, Billy-Dee and Stevo will be giving away tickets to the Rick Raven concert, so make sure you're up early and tuned in to the Morning Show for your chance to win. Rick Raven - doing it live in December for FM 114.9. Got some Aerosmith for you soon with 'Angel,' and Natalie's up next with the news - on the hour, every hour at your home of real rock 'n' roll, FM 114.9'

A feeling of satisfaction washed over Nat and he smiled.

'The Montgomery's have been farming oysters for gener- ations. Young Richard's gonna carry on that tradition - he's an oyster farmer, not a guitar player.'

'Yeah right,' said Nat, recalling Wayne Montgomery's comments from a few years ago.

'Dad? Did you say something?' asked Hanna.

'Here's to oyster farmers,' he replied, raising his hot mug of coffee in the air. Seeing the confused look on Hanna's face, he added, 'I just remembered something, is all. Hey, we're nearly at the airport. Hopefully, we can get a car park close to the terminal.'

After a long flight, the weary travellers fell asleep on the car journey home, including Hanna, who claimed she hadn't slept well because Snuffles kept moving on her bed.

Upon returning to the Baxter residence, Alana greeted their Swedish friends with a warm welcome. While she was preparing lunch, Nat snuck out to the car and gathered the daffodils, along with champagne, some almond nougat, and a box of orange chocolates. Nat was, in fact, the orange choco- late fan, and Alana knew she'd have to hide them, or else he'd consume them all!

Alana's eyes widened when she saw the gifts, and she gave her husband a giant hug! Nathan also presented her with a pair of handcrafted coffee mugs delicately nestled in a small wooden box. These mugs, crafted by Concordia, were adorned with a sunshine-yellow daffodil on each. The ceramic art pieces were exquisite, leaving Alana - aware of the floral significance, teary-eyed. Brigitta also took a liking to them and requested a visit to Concordia's studio to acquire something for their home in Linköping. After a few hours of afternoon rest, both families went to the Southern Anchor for a dual-celebration dinner. Nat was delighted to have his old friends there to celebrate his tenth wedding anniversary, and combining it with a 'welcome party' for them made the occasion truly special. After dinner, Baxter and Edvard sat on Nat's back verandah, drinking beer and admiring the stars. Nat had speakers rigged up to his stereo inside the house, and the sound echoed loudly throughout the area.

'What's it gonna be, brother? Eric or George?' asked Ed, rifling through Baxter's large record collection.

'You're the guest, so the choice is yours,' replied Nat. The first strains of 'Motherless Children' echoed out from the speakers, much to Baxter's delight.

'A fine choice, Edwardo, a fine choice indeed,' he uttered, referencing the opening track on Eric Clapton's *461 Ocean Boulevard* album. 'You know me well,' he added, starting to feel tipsy. Baxter emptied a fresh bottle of Ashton Ale into Ed's glass and looked over at his friend.

'It really is great to see you, brother.' They nodded and grinned, raised their glasses, and took in large gulps of cold beer. Edvard let out a contented 'ahh' before getting to his feet.

'I know what we need. What we need is a song,' he suggested.

'Great idea!' agreed Baxter. 'But let's get the guitars out after side one has finished. I've always loved Yvonne Elliman's vocals on 'I Shot The Sheriff,' and in fact, any day I hear them… is a good day.'

'What are you two trouble makers up to?' laughed Brigitta, dancing onto the verandah while singing Elliman's 1977 hit 'If I Can't Have You.' Alana and the kids followed close by, as an animated Brigitta danced near Ed.

'You've got great style there,' Alana said to her.

'Good music moves me,' replied Brigitta in her thick Swedish accent. The drink flowed and the guitars were brought out, along with a tambourine that Hanna played. Nat scurried into his music room to grab an acoustic bass for Erik to sling over his shoulder, while Alana and Brigitta nursed wine glasses and handled background harmonies. The Baxter and Håkansson clans joined in on a run-through of Neil Young's 'Come A Time,' 'Mull of Kintyre,' by Wings and a boisterous take of The Beatles' 'I Want To Hold Your Hand.' Following the third number, they all cheered noisily, pleased with their collective effort.

'You're right, Ed, he's a chip off the old block,' said Nat, praising Erik and his bass-playing.

'Thanks, Nat,' said Erik, who smiled shyly. 'My Dad's a great teacher. Y'know, I'm so jealous of the time period in which you two grew up; there were so many great bands around.'

'Yes, there was,' agreed Nat. 'We were lucky to have grown up with bands like The Beatles. There have been many wonderful songwriters, but Lennon and McCartney were on another level. Hey, did you know your Dad and I co-wrote a song together when I was in Gothenburg?'

Erik shook his head.

'That's right, we did! Oh man, I forgot all about that,' said Edvard. 'It was a half-decent song, but we never finished it.'

'Well, let's try and complete it before you return home,' suggested Baxter, getting to his feet. 'And we can demo it on my 4-track recorder as well!'

'Great idea, brother. I'm down with that,' replied Ed, excitedly.

After a couple of hours, Erik was hit by jet lag and he went to bed. Hanna, who had taken Button and Snuffles for an extra-long walk on the beach after dinner, also turned in, feeling tired.

Wanting to take advantage of the atmosphere and hopefully capture some creativity, the reunited musical duo of Håkansson and Baxter, armed with re-tuned guitars and recharged glasses - got straight to work. Brigitta and Alana sat together, watching as Nat and Ed laughed, hummed, worked on melodies, and scrawled down ideas. To everyone's amazement, Nat even brought out some half-finished lyrics in the very same notebook he'd had in Gothenburg! Memories flooded back as Edvard strummed, looked at Nathan, and sang the chorus. Baxter loved it: the chemistry, combined with that feeling of familiarity. He was nineteen years old again and it was a moment to savour.

'Tid är dyrbart,' said Alana, reading the song title over Nat's shoulder. 'What does that mean?'

'The English translation of 'Tid är dyrbart' is 'Time is precious,' explained Edvard.

'I really like that,' said Brigitta, 'It's about living in the now and appreciating what we have. When I was a small child, my mother would say that phrase to me.' The pretty blonde Swede took a small sip of wine before continuing. 'Watching you two create music again is magical. I can remember you both working on this song in our apartment in Gothenburg. Edvard, what are the rest of the lyrics?'

'Man, there's some great stuff in here,' he replied, reading from the notebook. He was silent as he read the words and nodded. 'There's some meaningful lines in here about what you need to be happy. It talks about love, music, harmony, friendship, and chances.'

'Here's to friendship,' said Brigitta, drunkenly clinking her glass with the others.

'Here's to chances,' chimed Ed, raising his beer.

'....and here's to second chances,' said Nat, locking eyes with Alana, who smiled.

Nathan encourages you to search out some of the songs mentioned in Sea Spray. Music - the elixir of life!

Aerosmith: *Angel, Chip Away The Stone*

America: *A Horse With No Name, Ventura Highway*

Nathan Baxter: *Alana*

The Babys: *Isn't It Time*

Joan Baez: *Diamonds and Rust, The Night They Drove Old Dixie Down*

Beatles: *A Day In The Life, And I Love Her, Blackbird, Eight Days A Week, Hey Jude, I'll Be Back, I'll Follow The Sun, In My Life, I Want To Hold Your Hand, While My Guitar Gently Weeps, Yer Blues*

Chuck Berry: *School Days*

Blind Faith: *Well Alright, Under My Thumb, Can't Find My Way Home*

Blue Öyster Cult: *(Don't Fear) The Reaper*

Bread: *Make It With You*

Carpenters: *Solitaire*

Cheap Trick: *Surrender*

Eric Clapton: *Cocaine, Give Me Strength, I Shot The Sheriff, Let It Grow, Mainline Florida, Motherless Children*

Dave Clarke Five: *Glad All Over*

Cris T. Collins: *Falling Apart With A Shattered Heart*

Cream: *Spoonful, White Room*

Derek and the Dominos: *Layla*

Bob Dylan: *Forever Young*

Eagles: *Already Gone, Hotel California*

Yvonne Elliman: *Can't Find My Way Home, If I Can't Have You*

Fleetwood Mac: *Rhiannon*

George Harrison: *Ding Dong, Give Me Love (Give Me Peace on Earth), My Sweet Lord*

Jimi Hendrix: *All Along The Watchtower, Angel, Foxy Lady, Hey Joe*

Jefferson Airplane: *White Rabbit*

Journey: *Wheel In The Sky*

Kinks: *Celluloid Heroes*

Kiss: *Hard Luck Woman*

John Lennon: *Imagine, Love, Working Class Hero*

Lynyrd Skynyrd: *Simple Man*

Monkees: *(I'm Not Your) Steppin' Stone*

Nathan and The Nighthawks: *Pristine Heart, Vanilla Stars*

Ted Nugent: *Stranglehold, Cat Scratch Fever*

Off Course: *Sayonara*

Pink Floyd: *Wish You Were Here*

Queen: *Crazy Little Thing Called Love*

Rainbow: *Man On The Silver Mountain*

Rick Raven: *Starlight*

Rolling Stones: *Angie, Heart of Stone, Respectable, Satisfaction, Wild Horses*

Demis Roussos: *Forever and Ever, Paperback Writer*

The Sea Fleas: *Lovesick Sailor*

Simon & Garfunkel: *The Sound of Silence*

Rod Stewart: *Mandolin Wind*

James Taylor: *Fire and Rain*

UFO: *Doctor Doctor, Rock Bottom*

Gene Vincent: *Be-Bop-A-Lula*

Joe Walsh: *Rocky Mountain Way*

Bob Welch: *Ebony Eyes*

The Who: *Behind Blue Eyes, Won't Get Fooled Again*

Mason Williams: *Classical Gas*

Wings: *Junior's Farm, Mull of Kintyre, Old Siam Sir*

Neil Young: *Cinnamon Girl, Comes A Time, Heart of Gold, Old Man*

LISEBERGS
KONSERTHALL
I afton kl. 19.30
SBA presenterar

BLIND
FAITH
CLAPTON
WINWOOD
BAKER/GRECH
BABYLON

Bilj. I Lisebergs kassa
o. tidningscentralerna.

KONSERTHALLEN, LISEBERG

Onsdagen den 18 juni kl. 19.30

BLIND FAITH

PARKETT

HÖGER

Pris kr 19:—

+ sedvanlig entré till parken.

Bänk 7

Plats 4

Shop Assistant: Busy city store seeks honest, reliable hard worker . suit student.No experience necessary. Transton's Toys - 848-2547

Music Teacher Wanted, immediate start, preferably skilled in piano or guitar. Good pay and working conditions, only qualified teachers need apply. Clare High School. Telephone: 851-5412.

Mechanic wanted to join our workshop. Must be skilled in repairs and maintenance of various vehicles. Call Colin 848-2336

Denis R. Gray was born in Sydney but calls the Canberra region home. He draws inspiration from his own life experiences and love for music. Although he often dips his toe in the waters of the modern world, Denis finds solace in living in the past surrounded by his book and record collection. When he's not writing, Denis enjoys riding motorcycles, collecting records, and reading. This is his second book.

Also by the author:
Movin' On: A Teenage Poet, a Small Town, a Big Dream
ISBN: 978-0-6489302-1-1